Now and Zen

D1607783

Also by Deb Lewis and Pat Ondarko

NOVELS

Bad to The Last Drop

Too Much at Stake

Now and Zen

Deb Lewis and Pat Ondarko

Little Big Bay LLC

LITTLE PLACE ~ BIG IDEAS ~ ON THE BAY

www.littlebigbay.com

Now and Zen

For information: www.bestfriendsmysteries.com

Authors: Deb Lewis and Pat Ondarko

Book editor: Catherine Lange

Book design: Roslyn Nelson

Cover design: Pat Ondarko

Author photo: Carol Seago

Island map: Holly Marie Tourdot

La Pointe map: Madeline Island Ferry Line

Printed in the United States of America

ISBN 978-0-9834330-6-4
Library of Congress Control Number: 2012936348

Publisher: Little Big Bay LLC
littlebigbay.com

TO YOU, OUR READERS

GREETINGS!

As you may have noticed, our *Best Friends Series* has taken you through the seasons. *Bad to the Last Drop* was set deep in the snow banks of winter. *Too Much at Stake* arrived with the greening of spring. *Now and Zen,* the one you hold in your hands, brings you into the heat of summer on the big lake.

In this installment, we take you to Madeline Island, another of our favorite places. Madeline Island is located in Lake Superior about two miles offshore from Bayfield, Wisconsin. You can travel from Bayfield to Madeline Island seasonally by ferry or an ice road, if you can believe it. Now that's a fun adventure if you're ever in the area in winter! Madeline Island is the traditional spiritual center of the Lake Superior Ojibwe and was one of the earliest settlements in the area.

We just love to leave our families behind and go to "the island" to get away from it all as often as we can.

What will the turning of the leaves look like in northern Wisconsin? Watch for our next book, *Murder on the Bridge.* In it, you'll get to know two delightful older women named Jessie and Millie, who go on a bridge tournament cruise to have some fun. As it turns out, bridge is not the only thing on the ship's daily manifest. Don't worry. We will be back in the future for another *Best Friends* Mystery.

We hope you enjoy the reading as much as we enjoyed the writing.

Deb and Pat
Wisconsin, 2012

DEDICATED TO

The International Council

of Thirteen Indigenous Grandmothers

and grandmothers everywhere

who, no matter their religious belief,

know intrinsically that light and dark

are as real as the sun and the moon.

And who also know that the light

will always be stronger because

of the power called love.

Prologue

The day the woman disappeared, Captain Mike got up early and took his two black labs out for a run.

Just like he always did.

He ate his oatmeal, grabbed his thermos of hot coffee, and kissed his wife absentmindedly.

Just like he always did.

Checking the sky for weather, he started to get into his old red Ford pickup.

Just like he always did.

On this day, he noticed a mature female eagle overhead and stopped for a moment to follow her flight as she soared, riding the winds off the big lake. Breathing in deeply the scent of water and sand, and still captivated by her, he watched in awe as she dipped to water's edge, effortlessly picking up a large whitefish.

What might it be like, he thought enviously, *to fly with those great powerful wings on the currents like she does?*

Smiling, he started his old truck. Turning left, he headed to the lake and his Island Queen Ferry, parked at the Bayfield dock. He was eager to get the old girl out and fly, in his own way, on the waves of Lake Superior. Twenty-three years as ferry captain, and his heart still beat a bit faster at the thought.

Just like it always did.

But this day wasn't any other day. It was an ordinary day turned extraordinary by one single event. This was the day in which what he "always did" changed forever.

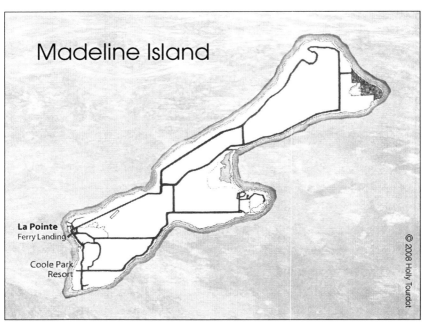

Madeline Island

La Pointe
Ferry Landing

Coole Park
Resort

© 2008 Holly Tourdot

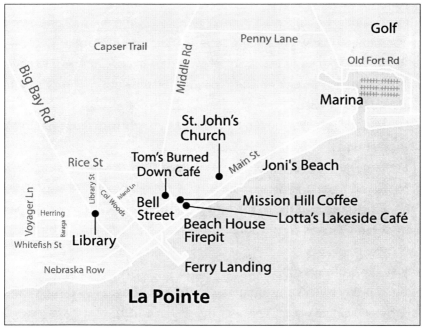

Golf

Capser Trail

Penny Lane

Middle Rd

Old Fort Rd

Big Bay Rd

Marina

St. John's
Church

Rice St

Tom's Burned
Down Café

Main St

Joni's Beach

Voyager Ln

Library St

Col Woods

Island Ln

Bell
Street

Mission Hill Coffee

Herring

Baraga

Beach House
Firepit

Lotta's Lakeside Café

Whitefish St

Library

Nebraska Row

Ferry Landing

La Pointe

Chapter One
June 20

Staring blankly at the open suitcase on the bed in front of her, Deb Linberg's thoughts drifted from the task at hand. She knew that the plan she and her best friend Pat Kerry had set in motion two months ago for a women's retreat on Madeline Island matched the dream they'd been hatching for years. Yet she was worried.

Do we spend our lives just frantically chasing dreams? she wondered, feeling a certain peril in the approaching test of making this dream of an island retreat come true. *This dream feels like it's still stuck in the dead of night.*

"Wake up, Deb!" she said to herself out loud. She laughed at herself, shaking her head.

First things first, if I'm going to pick up Pat on time.

She started ticking off a checklist on her fingers.

Candles, bottle of wine, bath oil, tie dyed shirt, underwear, white blouse, sandals, journal. She threw each item in turn into her overnight bag.

What about toothpaste? I can't take the only tube in the house. Pat will have toothpaste I can use.

"A good book? Nope. No time for reading on this trip. Now, where is my cell, anyway?"

"Cliffy, can you come here for a minute?"

"What, Mom?"

"It's time to play the phone game, hon. You know the drill. I'm going to dial my cell phone. You listen for the ring, and go find it for me."

"Okay, Mom," Cliffy replied, a wide smile on his face. He was so eager to please, this youngest of her six.

"Oh, and Mom, just thought you'd like to know," he said, popping his head back in the door, "you were talking out loud to yourself again."

"Rats, pretty soon I'll be like Gram," she said out loud and then covered her mouth quickly to stop herself.

She dialed and heard a ringing in a distant room.

"Here it is, Mom," Cliffy said breathlessly as he tossed the cell on the bed.

"Thanks, love. What would I do without you?" Deb smiled at him, mussing his hair.

Nice having a kid who still lets me do that, she thought.

Cliffy beamed, his big brown eyes shining.

"Is that all? I'm playing my new video game, and Mom? Don't mess my hair like that in front of Gene, okay?"

She nodded and sighed. *They grow up so fast.*

Deb zipped her bag and dragged it down the stairs, eager to get on the road.

"I have to go, boys," she called cheerfully. "The ferry waits for no one. Pat and I have to get out to Madeline Island early to set up for the party... I mean... retreat."

Deb's husband Marc was intently reading his newspaper at the break-fast table while their son Eugene was busy reading the comics. No one seemed interested in her departure.

"See you in a few days," Marc replied, without looking up.

"Party? Can we come?" Eugene asked, belatedly registering her mis-spoken words.

"Sorry, my boy. Not this time. I promise we'll make a trip together yet this summer. This is girl time," she said, patting him on the shoulder. After kissing them all and stroking Strider, her golden retriever, Deb heaved her bag up to her shoulder and swung the door open with her foot.

Clicking the control on her keys, the trunk of her new red convertible opened like magic. It had been a gift from Marc over a year earlier after she and Pat had solved the mystery behind an unexpected death at Lake

Superior Big Top Chautauqua. Marc had gifted the car after Deb and Pat had solved the mystery before the police managed to. Marc secretly hoped her new toy would keep Deb busy and away from any more dangerous adventures.

Deb smiled at the memory of the gift. Then she giggled out loud. Almost sixty and married over twenty-five years, she still got the tingles whenever Marc came home early from sailing or work. Even so, they found little time to be alone since adopting their two youngest.

Starting the car, she tooted goodbye to her boys and her cares.

Flipping through the TV channels while waiting for Deb, Pat looked for the weather report to see the forecast for the retreat. She stopped on channel ten, where a news report caught her ear.

"The most amazing thing," the reporter said, "is happening on the South Shore. You see behind me as I speak, live coverage of heavy traffic moving east towards Bayfield from Duluth, and..." Just then the phone rang.

"Dang," Pat said, turning off the T.V. *Oh, it's Martin.* Pat thought, standing by the window and watching for Deb. *I'd better take this call.*

"Mom, I'm so glad I caught you."

"What? The girls aren't coming?" Pat interrupted.

"No, no, Mom, they're coming. I just have to tell you something. It's important, listen..."

Just then, Pat heard a loud rendition of *Riding The Wind*, a Big Top Chautauqua tune, coming from Deb's car horn in the driveway. "Sorry, Martin, it'll have to wait. I'll call you later. Love you." Hanging up the cell, Pat ran quickly out the door.

Deb giggled at the sound of the horn.

Tall, strong, small-waisted but Rubenesque, Deb didn't need to be seated in a sporty red Miata for men to flirt with her. Short-cropped strawberry blond hair, a button nose, freckles, and curious blue eyes that get lost in the wrinkles at their corners when she laughs all cast her as the likeable woman next door who draws you in, invites your confidences, and tricks you into revealing your innermost self. And behind that welcoming face, a lawyer's mind that suits her profession well.

Pat came quickly out the back door with a skip in her step, carrying her small overnight bag.

If you didn't look closely at Pat, you might only see an older lady's chunky body and cheaply cut clothes. But look into Pat's dark brown eyes, and you see the gypsy who leads two lives. The first, as an in-charge Lutheran pastor, who started out being a collar wearer, mainly to remind herself who she was supposed to be. The other, as a yearner, a cynic with a deep need to know the truth at all cost, a trait that sometimes gets her into hot water in her first life.

The gypsy-eyed Pat had recently decided quite firmly that if she had a choice between happy or sad, she would pick happy. And so she did.

"Packing light as usual, I see!" Deb said gaily. "Roof up or down today?"

"Is there any question? How will we ever hear that fancy new horn if we don't?" Pat replied, squinting up into the bright morning sun. She put on her sunglasses. "We're going to the island. Down, of course!"

Tossing her satchel into the popped trunk, Pat slid easily into the front seat. Meanwhile, Deb was busy pushing buttons on the dash.

"Wish I could remember how to do this," she mumbled. "I have to look up the directions every time."

Pat reached into the glove compartment for the manual.

The canvas roof began to lift up from the top front of the windshield and to fold accordion style toward the back seat. Suddenly it stopped with a whooo... wheee... crunch. Whooo... wheee... crunch.

"What's the matter with this darn thing?" Deb asked with annoyance, noticing Pat's neighbors watching them from the yard across the street. She waved, and they smiled and waved back.

"It's stuck!" she said grumpily, glancing with embarrassment at the half-raised roof sticking straight into the air as the motor ground over and over. "Maybe if I just push *this* button..." Suddenly, the strains of Van Morrison filled the whole street. "Help," she said, looking at Pat and frantically pushing one button and then another. Soon the windshield wipers were going to the beat and the lights were blinking off and on, and the neighbors were visibly laughing. Other doors were starting to open around them.

Better than going to the circus, Pat thought, trying to keep herself from laughing and handing the manual to Deb.

"We have to hurry. The ferry only leaves Bayfield every half hour and we have some signs to put up. We want to get there before our friends so they can find us," Deb wailed.

"Here, I can do it. Let me help," Pat replied, standing up and giving the roof a swift push.

"Wait a minute! This is my new car."

Amazingly, the roof came unstuck and slid down with a satisfying bang.

"Sunny skies all around," Pat said gaily, settling back into her seat and putting on her seat belt. "Nothing but a relaxing retreat in front of us."

Deb took a deep breath and started to drive away.

"You might want to turn off the alarm system and radio," Pat added. She waved to the neighbors, who, still laughing, turned to go into their houses.

It was just another day in a small town.

Chapter Two
April 15

The idea for a women's gathering hatched a few months previously, while Pat sat waiting for Deb to arrive for lunch at the Second Street Bistro in Ashland.

The waiter set down a cup of French roast and took away Pat's wine glass, emptied now of her favorite Pinot Grigio. She'd been savoring the wine when the idea popped unexpectedly into her mind.

As Deb sat down, Pat said, "Do you think we'll ever have a retreat center like we dreamed about?"

"Can't have it unless you dream it," Deb said, smiling, giving Pat back an answer she'd received often enough from Pat.

"True enough," Pat replied.

Then Deb's face became serious. "Truth is, we can do it if we really want to. The boys will be out of the house in..." She counted on her fingers, "...in four years. Four years!" she groaned.

"Oh, I know, but no matter how we look at it, we could never afford a place big enough on Madeline Island."

"Don't be too sure. Remember what my counselor told me when I was deciding whether to give up my law practice or not," Deb said. Lay out a plan like a business plan for the next year or two, she said. What would it look like?" It helped then."

Deb reached for her coffee mug and glanced down at her Paraguayan sweater.

"We could do that," she added as she took a sip of coffee. "After all, I got to Paraguay, didn't I?"

"Doesn't matter. Crunch the numbers," Pat sighed with resignation. "Think of the backers we would need. We could never afford it. We'd have to kill off our husbands for the insurance money." She leaned her elbows on the table and looked off in the distance. "Of course, we'd have to make darn sure there was enough money in the policies before we went to such extremes."

"I heard that, ladies. No planning murders in my place. It's bad for business. Besides, I thought you two solved murders, not committed them," called the waiter, as he hurried by with an order.

"Stop that! I don't even like to hear you joke about it. But you're right about the money." Deb sighed, in agreement. "We'd have to win the lottery. What would it cost, do you think, five hundred thousand?"

"Just for starters," Pat agreed gloomily. "Then there's fix-up costs, maintenance, a gardener, a masseuse – you know we would need one – and a cook."

"Even if we did all that ourselves, there'd be no time to enjoy the place, or our guests. We'd be like the chef who never gets to enjoy a great sit-down meal."

"Too bad. If it weren't for the initial outlay for the building and property, we could probably make a go of it." Pat conceded.

Deb looked up.

"Why do we have to?" she asked.

"Have to what? Wait a minute... I know that look. I've seen it before. It's like you have a light bulb shining above your head. You've gone and had one of your brilliant ideas, and it isn't even..." She looked up at the clock on the wall. "... twelve thirty yet."

"No, just listen," Deb insisted. "Why do we have to have a building at all? There are plenty of inexpensive meeting places on the island. Lots of bed and breakfasts, a church or two, and rentals. We wouldn't have to run it all year round. We could do a theme retreat once or twice a year. It would be great. Just think of it. And we wouldn't have to wait for the kids to leave home either."

"You're the one who has to worry about the kid thing. I sent ours packing long ago." Pat was quiet for a moment, a good sign as far as Deb was concerned, because she knew Pat was actually considering it.

"Mmm... No buildings? What about meals, or, you know," Pat replied, picking up on her friend's enthusiasm, "you're right. I'll bet we could even use the beach on the shoreline for a bonfire at night."

"Speakers could be at churches or the library. We could keep the costs down. Ask for volunteers. Heck, our friends would love to help us. Restaurants would likely give us a discount when we bring in twenty or thirty people. You know the music camp must do it that way every summer. Let's find out."

Excited by their discussion, Deb didn't even notice she had spilled coffee down the front of her favorite sweater.

"If you build it, they will come," she said grandly, referring to a line from *Field of Dreams,* one of her all-time favorite baseball movies. She waved her fingers at the waiter to get his attention. "This calls for a celebration. Would you bring us two glasses of the house Chablis with our lunch?"

He nodded his head.

"As long as you're not really celebrating your husbands' demises," he replied.

"Heck, no. We figured out a better way." Deb turned to Pat. "So, what kind of retreat theme? Feminism... art?"

"No, something more 'woo woo.' If we're going out on a limb, let's really do something fun! I know! They've been making so much about the end of the Mayan calendar in the news, you know, end of the world stuff. Let's do a summer solstice retreat. A rebirth kind of thing, starting with Tai Chi in the morning and ending with a solstice bonfire and party."

"What? Are you talking this year?" Deb asked dubiously. "Solstice is only a few months away."

Pat waved away her objections like she was swatting at a mosquito.

"No big deal. It's not like the first one will be for a hundred people. We'll just invite friends and maybe family. Let's see, maybe thirty or so. Enough to get the discounts. Piece of cake."

"You always make things sound so easy, but why is it things never turn out that way?" Deb shook her head.

With most people, I can just daydream and enjoy ideas, Deb thought, *never really having to act on them.* With Pat, she dreams something and voila! It starts to become a reality. *What have I done?*

The waiter returned with filled glasses. Picking one up, Pat raised it in salute.

"A good friend once said, just a moment ago, something like: 'if you don't dream it, you can't have it.' Here's to a great dream becoming a reality."

"Okay, Lucy, this Ethel's in." Deb lifted her glass and clinked it with Pat's, and then took a steep swallow. "Here's to a retreat house without the house. Can't wait."

Here we go again, she thought.

Chapter Three
April 16

The very next day, the two best friends headed to the Bistro again, reveling in the rare freedom of a day to themselves.

Not everyone is lucky enough to have a best friend. People often say things like: 'my husband is my best friend,' or 'my mother is my best friend.' Though Pat and Deb love their family members like crazy and would die willingly for any one of them, they are *best* friends. No bones about it.

Feeling the welcome ambiance of the place, Pat and Deb followed a group of women into the large cozy room, which bustled with lunch crowd noise. Pat inhaled the intoxicating scent of homemade soup.

"Come on in!" the owner called from his perch behind the wine bar at the far end.

"Hi, Pat!" greeted a neighbor, who sat chatting amicably at the bar.

Deb recognized several other friends and neighbors in the large wooden booths hugging the red wall on the right.

"Hi, Pastor!" A smiling former parishioner called to Pat from his table in the front window.

"And then he said that the mayor had invited the Catholic priest to say the prayer at council meetings," Pat overheard a voice whispering conspiratorially. *Life goes on,* she thought as she passed by.

Pat glanced at the bright oil paintings on the wall to the left, the artistic flavor of the month.

"This place is better than reading a newspaper," Deb murmured.

"That's the deal with small towns," Pat said, as she slid into the cushioned booth nearest to the kitchen. "The good news is, everyone knows your business, and the bad news is… "

"Everyone knows your business!" Deb chimed in, as she picked up her menu.

"Hey ladies, good to see you back. Should I bring coffee or… ?" the waiter asked with a smile.

"Your wonderful coffee will be just fine. We're making up an invite and have to be clearheaded. What's the soup today?" Pat asked.

"Your favorite: wild mushroom. Want a big bowl?" Pat nodded.

"Me, too," Deb said. "And baguettes, please."

"Sure, what are you working on?"

In a small town, it is never impolite to be snoopy.

"A fund raiser?"

He was always up for helping out a good cause when he could.

"We're actually thinking, no, strike that, we're doing a women's retreat out on the island at summer solstice. Think your wife would like to come?"

"Solstice? Like a coven thing? What will you call it? Witches Unite? Take Back the Night?'"

"Not bad, but no cigar. It's kind of a renewal retreat, with a couple of workshops and a masseuse."

"A masseuse? Heck, with my wife, *I* could use a break."

"Sorry. No men at this one."

"Oh well, good luck then. The coffee is just brewing. I'll be back with it in a minute." He stopped at the next booth on the way to the kitchen. "Hello, anything to drink?"

"So, what do we want it to say?" Deb asked, getting down to business. "Let's make sure they don't think it's some kind of witch thing."

"Could be worse," Pat replied, pulling out her notebook and favorite pen. "After all, the women labeled as witches in the old days were by and large healers and spiritual leaders. How about 'Come for solstice and a cup of witch's brew?'" she teased.

"Forget it. My mom would never come with that title. How about, 'Come to the islands'?"

"That's a great play on words. It sounds like Maui," Pat said, writing it down. "But off the record, I know some of our relatives would qualify to come to a coven of the fabled kind, broomsticks and all."

"Isn't that the truth! Wasn't Maui wonderful?" Deb asked dreamily. "Wouldn't it be great if we could have our retreat there?"

"Focus! We need to get this invitation out in the next few days." Pat looked up from her writing at Deb. "And yes, it was wonderful. And yes, maybe if these retreats work out, next year we can do Maui. The other island." They both laughed.

Pat scribbled feverishly for a few minutes and then turned a messy page towards Deb. "How does this look?"

COME TO THE ISLAND!!
YOU ARE INVITED TO A SOLSTICE RETREAT

Okay, Okay, It's not to Jamaica or to Hawaii.
It's to Madeline Island and it won't be the same without you.

COME FOR JUST THE DAY OF THE UPCOMING SUMMER SOLSTICE,
OR COME FOR ALL FOUR DAYS.

This is a chance for sisters to be together.
And if you got this invite, we consider you our sister.
There will be book discussions, croquet, and wine.
And of course, a Solstice bonfire, which we hope to make
an annual tradition.
Find a schedule of speakers and events, plus places
for lodging, listed on the back.
Leave the men and kids at home, and join us for women's time.

HOPING YOU'LL BE WITH US,
Pat and Deb
Let us know if you're coming (or not). We'll be on Island time!

"Here's your coffee. Soup will be up in a few minutes." The waiter put down the steaming cups and hurried away to seat a couple at the door.

Stirring in a dollop of cream, Deb scrutinized the writing. "It looks good. We better have real dates and times on it, though, so there's no confusion. I love the list of speakers on the back. Now we just have to have some. Any ideas?"

Taking the paper, Pat added the dates.

"How's that? As for the speakers, I made a list. Here." She pulled a list out of her coat pocket.

"Jeeze, where did you find this piece of paper? I'm just glad you didn't write it on a used Kleenex." Reading the list more closely, Deb set down her spoon. "Hey, this says you and I and mostly our friends will be the speakers. What's with that?" she asked.

"Low overhead. Plus it's a way to get them there."

"Always thinking. Do you have something for our daughters to do? I'd love to have them there. Lately, they are so busy. Remember when they just loved to do things with us?"

"Yup, when they were about three, wasn't it? Pat said sarcastically. "I suppose we can somehow try to guilt them into it. Let me think on it."

"Good luck with that. Well, we've always got our granddaughters. Let's invite the little ones, too."

"Soup's on."

A waitress set down two big bowls and a basket of bread. Deb picked up her spoon and dipped it into the great bowl of steaming soup. Pushing their papers aside, the women dug in.

And so, it had all begun.

Chapter Four
April 18

A few days after their planning sessions at the Bistro, Pat was seated in her dining room across the antique table from Deb.

"Where are we tonight? Maui? Tahiti? Jamaica, perhaps?" Deb asked.

They were admiring the well-set table before them. Bone china, real silverware, and crystal goblets with blue plaid napkins folded in fan shapes created an elegant tableau.

Marc emerged from the kitchen, carrying a pitcher of frozen Margarita mix.

"Ladies, can I pour?" Deb and Pat stared at each other in amazement.

Men sometimes believe women dream about bedroom fantasies. They don't understand that real women dream about husbands cooking for them.

"Sure," Pat said. "Fill 'er up."

"Enjoy!" Marc said with a smile, backing out of the room. "Dinner will be ready in about ten minutes."

As Marc returned to the kitchen, an aroma of fried onions and red peppers permeated the air. They reached for their drinks and kicked off their shoes.

"This is the life," Deb said happily.

"What do you think they want?" Pat wondered aloud.

"Don't care," Deb answered. "This is worth a good roll in the hay."

Pat nodded in agreement.

A minute later, Pat's husband, Mitch, emerged with a white dish towel tied around his waist, carrying a tray of salsa and taco chips.

"Mmmm... looks great. What's the main course? Grilled chicken again?" Pat asked.

"Nope," Mitch said with a smirk on his face. "Real men cook Tex-Mex."

Deb reached over and pinched Pat.

"Who are these men, and can we keep them?"

Pat just looked at her with dazed amazement.

"Did Mitch go to cooking school this year while he was spending all that time in the city?" Deb asked. "I never knew he had it in him."

"He still surprises me after all these years," Pat replied. "Most people sleepwalk their way through life doing whatever is easiest."

"Yeah, yeah, but how did you really get him to do it? Drug him?"

Hearing banging in the kitchen, the women sat quietly. Pat grabbed some chips and scooped them into the salsa.

"Great salsa! Did Marc make it?"

"Oh, you know he makes the best homemade salsa there is."

Mitch wasn't the only person full of surprises. Pat and Deb had surprised themselves by being drawn into solving two local murders in the previous few years. Close encounters with death had made them treasure the simple pleasures of daily life. Simple gifts like husbands who cook. Men who not only cook, but who knock themselves out trying.

Life is so good, Deb thought. As if reading her mind, Pat nodded.

"It sure was nice of Mitch to invite us to dinner. What's the occasion, anyway? It's not a special day, is it? Did I forget a birthday again?"

"Nope," Pat replied, "guys! After Marc bought you a Miata, Mitch decided he wouldn't be outdone. He just made up his mind he would learn to cook my favorite foods, and here we are!" They both giggled. Pat raised her glass in a silent toast to these loyal men in their lives.

"How are we going to tell them about our retreat?" Deb wondered uneasily.

"You know we always find a way," Pat said with a wink.

Half an hour later, the two couples sat happily enjoying plates laden with dirty rice, grilled veggies and topped with chocolate mole sauce. Deb smiled at Mitch.

"Mitch, I have to hand it to you. You really have outdone yourself. We'll have to put this recipe in our next cookbook. How on earth did you do this, anyway?" She rubbed her too full stomach.

"Just something I whipped up," he replied mysteriously. "Besides, I have to find some way to keep you two around once in awhile. Especially after the trips you have made together to Nevis and Canada the past few years.

"You mean you really like having me around?" Pat asked.

"Sure. Marc and I were talking in the kitchen, and we think the next trip should include us."

"Well, maybe not the next one. But for sure the one after that!" Deb said sheepishly. "As a matter of fact, we've been meaning to talk to you about something."

"Here we go," Marc said. "Another adventure for the Bobbsey Twins. Let's hear what's up this time. Where are you going now? Wait a minute. Pass the pitcher over here first before you tell me," he continued, gesturing to the Margarita mix.

Deb smiled at her tolerant husband, as she filled up his glass.

"We're just going on a little retreat," Pat said.

"Where to this time?" Mitch asked. "You're not going back to Paraguay with Deb are you?"

"Not that far. Just over to Madeline Island," Deb replied gaily, noticing the obvious relief on the men's faces. "We wanted to spend summer solstice with the important women in our lives. So we're inviting a few of them to come with us. Just our close circle. You know, our moms, daughters, granddaughters, and a few friends. We'd invite you, but it's just going to be a girls' weekend away.

"Do you really think you can get them all to come?" Marc asked skeptically.

"If you plan it, they will come," Deb replied, catching Pat's eye.

The two men looked at each other with a knowing glance.

Mitch leaned over to Marc and whispered into his ear.

"What do you bet that this ends up costing us money?"

Chapter Five
April 19

The next day, one of Pat's rare attempts at housework was interrupted by the ringing of her cell. She turned off the vacuum and heard a familiar voice.

"Hi, Mom. How are things going?" Pat sat down for a good chat. She always loved when her son called.

"Good, good. How are all my wild babies down there?" Martin had moved his wife and their little family to Houston to take a job managing a lab at Baylor Medical School. Everyone thought it would be a short-term stay. They had been there for eight years.

Too far for grandbabies, Pat thought.

"Busy as usual with both girls in school. JoJo's going to preschool two mornings a week." There was a pause. "So we got your invite."

"I know, don't think I thought you and the girls could come. I just sent it so your wife could see it," Pat replied.

"Well, the thing is, she just might be able to come. Her mom wants us to come up for a family reunion, and it's just about the same time. Even so," he cautioned, "it's still two hundred miles to Madeline Island from Minneapolis."

Wow, thought Pat. Her mind began to scheme.

"You and JoJo could stay with Mitch at the house, and the girls could come, even if it was for only one night." Pat started to get excited. "I'll even pay for the room."

"Thanks, Mom. We'll see. Say, I showed the invitation to my team at work, and they thought it was a hoot. We had an extra half hour between lab classes so we started to put together a YouTube video just for fun. I thought you could let the people know that are coming, and they could watch it. What do you think?"

Pat had only half listened, her mind happily focused on the possibility of her granddaughters coming to the retreat.

"Sounds interesting. How would we watch it?"

Just then, there was a knock at the front door.

"Hold on. Someone's at the... oh, hi Deb," she called out. "Martin's on the phone and guess what? The girls might be able to come to our retreat. Isn't that great?" Pat gestured with a thumbs up sign.

"Hold your horses, Mom. I said maybe. Even if we're in Minnesota at the right time, it's still really busy when we're in town, you know." Pat could hear him trying to be diplomatic but clearly caught in the middle of trying to please everyone.

"Say, as long as you have Deb there," he continued, "could you use your new handy iPhone and do a little thing on it? That's really why I called. We thought we could put it on the YouTube site."

"Like what?" Pat motioned to Deb to stand closer so she could hear.

"Oh, something like your two faces smiling, with hats on and saying 'come to the island.' You could maybe do a little samba dance," he said hopefully. In the background they could hear muffled laughter.

"Is your team all listening to this?" Pat asked. "You are becoming more and more like your grandmother every day," she added with mock sternness. "And you guys listening; don't encourage him." More laughter erupted from the other end of the line. Secretly pleased at her son's silliness, she gave in.

"Right now? You want us to do it right now? I don't even know how to do it. Send it from my phone, I mean, not be silly. Lord knows I know how to do that."

"Like mother, like son. And Mom, for the record, you don't know how to do ninety percent of the stuff that iPhone can do. It'll be good for you to try. Just get a pen and write this down."

A few minutes later, Pat looked down at the page of instructions. She clicked off to the sound of "Love you, Mom." *All women should have a son,* she thought fondly. Pat turned to her friend.

"So I turn it on like this." She pressed the button. "And voila, we're on!"

"Wait a minute! We need to get the hats and decide what we're going to say."

"Here, you hold it. I'm afraid to turn it off. I might not get it going again. Say something witty," Pat called over her shoulder as she ran out of the room.

"Well, Martin, hope you can edit this out because your crazy mother has gone to get hats. Here she comes back," Deb said with relief in her voice.

"To Martin and the team at his crazy scientist's lab: First, I hope this makes it to you," Pat began. "We had this scheme, I mean, idea, to have a retreat for women at solstice, and here is my co-conspirator to tell you about it. Take it away, Deb." With that she turned the lens to her friend, who was donning a bright yellow Madeline Island all-weather hat.

"Pat, what are you doing?" Deb asked in anxious alarm. Pat made rolling motions with her hands, and smiled encouragingly.

"Hi," Deb began as she waved her hand. "If you're watching this, you already know I'm Deb. You probably have received your invite to experience summer solstice on the healing island of Madeline. You don't have to bring anything but a happy soul and a joyful heart. If you're missing either of those right now, don't worry. You'll find them if you come. Take it away Pat."

Startled, Pat turned the phone towards herself.

"Worried about the end of the Mayan calendar?" she improvised. "Want to spend solstice in a meaningful fun way? Join us. No work, no husbands, no worries." Moving right next to Deb so the phone would hopefully pick up both of their faces, she continued. "Bring your mom, bring your friend, bring your daughter if she's talking to you, but come; the island is calling." Deb started to giggle, but Pat began to sing slightly off key to a Jamaican beat:

Come to the island, don't worry about a t'ing .
Come to the island, catch onto your dream.
Come to the island, (Deb came in harmonizing)

Don't worry about a t'ing , come to the island,
Life can be more than it seems.

They laughed and did a little dance and the camera bounced around as Pat moved it.

"Sorry. I have to stop," she finally said, "because like a lot of women of a certain age, I laughed so hard, tears ran down my leg."

"Pat, you can't say that on YouTube," Deb said, laughing out loud.

"Have you ever seen YouTube? This is mild." Pat turned back to the screen. "Anyway, you're invited, so leave the kids and significant other at home and come." Waving, Pat touched the recorder off, and then pressed the buttons as instructed to send the video to her son.

"You didn't really send it?"

"Of course. Don't worry. Even if they do finish making it, which is doubtful, and then go to the bother of putting it online, no one will ever watch it."

She should have known better to say something like that. It was as if she had sent a challenge off to the universe. Though Pat and Deb usually pride themselves on being in charge of whatever they do, the Goddess, in the end, has always had a silly sense of humor.

Chapter Six
June 20

There goes a woman who is lucky, one might judge if one saw Deb driving down the road in a red Miata. After closely looking at the lines about her eyes or taking a moment to stop her and chat, one's initial impression might change to: *There goes a woman, who, in spite of life, has made her own good luck.*

On the way to the Bayfield dock, Deb carefully drove the speed limit through the little town of Washburn. She was always cautious of the ever-vigilant police officer. Spotting his car hiding in the weeds near the Sioux River north of town, Deb gave her horn a push and waved her hand at him. The strains of *Slow down, you move too fast* floated like incense through the air behind them. The officer stared stoically ahead as if he had heard it all before, biding his time until the next opportunity.

Half an hour later, in the heart of Bayfield, Deb pulled into the back of a long line of vehicles that stretched to the end of the ferry parking lot.

"Do you think we'll get on this time?" Pat worried aloud.

"Sure we will. This is peak season, but they have the big boat going, so there's plenty of space," Deb reassured.

As they pulled onto the ferry, the women noticed a trim, middle-aged man waving them forward to their resting spot on the deck. He tipped his ferry baseball hat towards them in recognition, revealing a tan and well-weathered bald head.

"Hi, Mike." Deb was on a first name basis with all the captains from her numerous trips to the island, but she knew Mike because of his long-time volunteer work in the community.

"Long line today," she continued, handing over their tickets. "Are you sure you can handle all this traffic?"

"We can always handle a flood of beautiful women taking a ride with us," Mike teased back, flashing a wide smile, framed by a neat, gray beard.

"Looks to me like the women are taking over out on the island today," he continued. "Guess it's just one of the perks of doing this job so many years."

"How many years has it been, anyway?" Deb asked.

"Twenty-three this September. I started back when I still had hair. And I still think it's the best job anyone could have."

"Don't you get tired of driving back and forth all day long?" Pat asked.

"No way. There's a whole lot more to this than just pushing automatic pilot. This is a huge operation that requires a lot of attention to detail," he pontificated. "Not to mention the responsibility for the lives and well being of customers. Transporting thousands of people across these waters is no picnic in the park. I think of this as a profession, not a job. In all my twenty-three years, we've only been late twice and never lost anyone yet!"

"That's quite a record!" Deb smiled at him. A horn honked impatiently behind them.

"Well, I better get this little hot rod on board so we don't ruin your record," she said.

"Have a great time," Mike replied, pointing to the next car. "good looking ride." he added.

Deb pulled into the indicated parking spot on the ferry, turned off the car and set the brake carefully. She stepped out to stretch her legs, patting the car's fender affectionately.

"Come on, Pat, let's go get a seat up top on the viewing deck," she urged.

Carrying her jacket and leading the way, Deb followed a long line of women to the narrow metal stairway. As she reached the top, her enthusiasm melted into disappointment when she saw that it was standing room only on the deck. Deb turned and found a place to stand along the railing.

A woman with dark eyes and hair approached them with a knowing smile.

"Are you Pat and Deb?" she asked with a hint of awe in her voice.

"Those are our names," Pat replied hesitantly. "But how do you know us? Have we met somewhere before?" A wrinkled furrow appeared on her brow.

"In a way we have," the woman replied mysteriously. "I'm Violet from Sedona. But most of my friends call me Windcatcher. I've come all this way to become more enlightened," she said in a throaty whisper.

Pat cocked her head sideways and glanced at Deb who raised her eyebrow.

"Do you have a relative on the island?" Deb asked.

"No, why would I?" Windcatcher replied, puzzled by the question. "Well, see you at solstice." After turning around in her gauzy dress, the stranger appeared to float away into the crowd.

"That was weird," Deb said.

Twenty minutes later as the ferry approached the dock, Pat was still standing on the top deck, looking out toward wild foliage surrounding the small town of La Pointe.

La Pointe, the mystical town where fairy tales could be centered, stands like a sentinel guarding her secrets on the mainland side of Madeline Island.

The view from La Pointe looks over toward the rolling hills of Bayfield, dotted with quaint shops, tall Victorian lady houses, and sailboats all in a row. The boats reminded Pat of heron legs stuck up in the air when they search with their bills for delectables in the muddy water bottom.

Standing on the dock, shimmering water in either direction hugs the shores of other islands or travels farther to the very place heaven touches earth at the water's edge on the horizon.

La Pointe herself is quite unlike any other place you may have traveled, though your eyes may tell you it is ordinary. There is magic there for certain special folks. One foot on her beach, one touch of toe to sand, one deep full breath of the moist air, and your heart knows. This is a place of magic in the capital M sense of the word... a place where you can dream and believe in those dreams... a place to become in... a place where time seems to stand still. Pat always felt as though she was coming home as she approached La Pointe on the ferry.

Some visitors may not sense the magic at all. They come to eat ice cream and visit the museum, smile politely, and go home thinking, *Well what a nice place to visit for a day.* With a slightly uneasy feeling, they quickly go back to their daily grind, with thoughts like *better get that lawn mowed; it's a busy day at work tomorrow.* These people are asleep to the unconditional gifts of respite and renewal offered to all guests of the island.

Pat took a deep breath and slowly let it out. *Even the air seems special out here,* she thought, *rarefied somehow, like what it must be in the Himalayas.*

She held onto the rail as the captain gently kissed the dock with the ferry.

Home. That's it. Madeline has the feel of home, she thought. The same feeling she got when she went back to her childhood home to Moccasin Lake in Chippewa National Forest, a place of belonging, nostalgia, and freedom.

A woman beside her bumped her arm while picking up her bag, bringing Pat out of her reverie.

"Oh, excuse me," Pat said with automatic Midwestern manners.

"No, no, it was me. Sorry." The woman glanced at Pat, and then looked again, smiling. "Do I know you?"

"Well, I have one of those ordinary faces." Pat smiled back. "Are you from Ashland?"

Since she had been a pastor in several states, Pat often ran into people who couldn't quite place where they had met her before. She rarely mentioned her church work because it usually stopped the conversation.

"No. Is that a town near here? I thought this town was Bayfield. Actually I've never been in Wisconsin, let alone to Madeline Island. Maybe it's just that you remind me of someone." The woman looked intently at Pat's face again and picked up her bag.

"Well, nice meeting you. I've got to find a motel. I hope I didn't make a mistake not pre-renting. Turning, she started down the metal stairs to the main deck.

As Pat walked towards the car, Deb approached her from behind.

"Hey, kiddo," Deb said, coming up behind her. "What do you say we stop off at Lotta's Lakeside Cafe for a good cup of coffee and a bagel before we check in?"

"Sure." Pat nodded her head in agreement. "You know I would never turn down a good cup of coffee."

Deb bent down to tie her shoelace. Losing her balance as she knelt, she fell clumsily onto the wood planking with a hard thud. Red-faced, Deb reached up to find her balance and was surprised to feel a warm hand in hers.

"Need some help?" a woman's voice sang light heartedly.

Deb looked up into the kindly face of a middle-aged stranger dressed in casual summer clothing. She peered intently into the woman's freckled face and piercing blue eyes, trying to place her.

Where do I know her from? Deb wondered, wracking her memory and lamenting her "senioritis."

The woman had a bemused, mirth-filled spark of recognition in her eyes. The corner of her mouth was raised in a half smile.

Deb reluctantly allowed the woman to help her regain her balance as she gracefully and effortlessly pulled her to her feet.

"Thanks," Deb said, "but that wasn't necessary."

"No problem," the woman replied. "After all, we women have to stick together at solstice time."

"Have we met?" Deb asked.

"I don't know, have we?"

"You just seem too familiar, like someone I've met before."

The woman, who was boarding the ferry, smiled, silently turned, and started walking toward the stairs to the top deck.

"Come on, Deb! We need to get our coffee. Let's get back down to your hot red 'lady' and blow this popsicle stand. I can't wait to hear what Lotta's going to say about that car."

"Sure, Pat," Deb said, turning and watching the woman walk away. "In a minute. I just had the strangest feeling being with that woman, just now. It was like when my teenage daughter told me after an argument, that, in spite of it all, she thought I was a good mother. I almost hate to leave her behind."

While Deb drove along the pier into La Pointe, they sat in companionable silence, quickly forgetting about the stranger.

The ferry was relatively empty on the trip back to Bayfield. Most of the traffic was going out to the island, so there were empty benches, but the woman who had helped Deb decided to go up to the top deck and stand anyway. She loved the lake and its breezes in her face. Halfway up the narrow metal stairs, a man bumped her hard as he pushed past. Startled, she grabbed the rail, her foot slipping dangerously.

Laughing too loudly to his male companion, he turned to stare at her for a moment. Realizing that she was a woman too old to be of interest, he forgot her immediately.

"Man, some people are slow when they get old." His friend gave her a sheepish grin, then moved on, claiming a bench for the two of them.

She sighed and continued up the stairs. As she walked toward the side of the boat, a woman reached out a hand.

"Are you alright? I saw what that guy did. What a weasel!"

"Oh, I'm fine," she replied. "It takes more than ill manners to change my mood. Besides, I find that what goes around comes around."

"Would you like to sit?" The woman patted the seat on the bench next to her and moved over.

"Thank you. I believe I will." She sat down and adjusted her shoe that had slipped off her heel.

"I sure hope that karma thing's not true. There are some things I've done I certainly don't want to be held accountable for." She laughed uncomfortably, surprised she had said anything at all.

"Oh, we all make mistakes, but what we do about them is what matters, don't you think?"

"You mean like if that guy had apologized just now? Although, some things you just can't make right by an 'I'm sorry.' I'm Lotta by the way, and you are?" she said, extending her hand.

"On my way to the mainland for a visit," the other said, deliberately misunderstanding.

Lotta nodded, not offended by the woman's aloofness. She, too, was used to keeping her own secrets.

Three benches over, two men were passing the time watching the other passengers.

"What about those two women over there?" the older one asked, nodding in their direction. He sat with his arms folded across his Armani covered belly like a big rich toad.

"Nah," the other replied, "too old for me." Unconsciously, his tongue slipped out, traveling over his lips as if he could taste them. "I like them young." He reached into his shirt pocket, pulled out a cigarette and lighter, and cupping his hands over his mouth, lit up.

"That's where you got it wrong. Now, the first one, I know her. That's Lotta, a tough cookie, and not someone to mess around with. I've heard rumors. But the other one; see how she carries herself so confidently? How well her clothes fit? Now that one has money; you can go to the bank on it."

"Money? Maybe so, but I like to keep business and pleasure separate."

The older man let out a cynical snort.

"In the dark it doesn't really matter, and the money can take you to a lot of warm places." He winked. Noticing the woman looking right into his eyes, he turned away, suddenly feeling ashamed and then angry, like a little boy caught stealing a cookie.

"You know that development project I was talking about?" the younger man asked, exhaling smoke from his cigarette. "I really do need some upfront cash." He glanced at his older companion. "And since it sounds like your cash cow may dry up, maybe I should rethink the business and pleasure thing."

Deep in his own thoughts, the older man was no longer listening.

Deb pulled up in front of the tiny cafe called Lottas.

"Come on, Deb," Pat said over her shoulder as she opened the door to the familiar tinkle of the doorbell. "Are you going to kiss that car every time you leave it like you do the kids?"

She stepped inside with sudden amazement. The room was filled with women of all ages. She looked around and spied one small open table close to the kitchen. They pulled out chairs just as a frazzled looking waitress came through the swinging kitchen doors. Smiling in recognition, she rushed by.

"Two veggie omelets, dry whole wheat, and a side of hummus. Do you want the hot sauce?" she asked, holding up the bottle. "Yell if you need anything."

Walking back to Pat and Deb's small table, the woman glanced around to make sure no one was waving for service.

"Hi, Sadie," Pat said.

"It's great to see you two. You certainly know how to throw a party." She poured them both coffees.

Deb looked up from the menu with a confused expression. "You mean some of our friends and family have already been showing up? I thought we'd be the first."

"Dang," Sadie said pulling up a chair from another table and straddling it. "If all these are family, your parents had some kind of sex life." She waved a hand at the crowded room.

"What are you talking about? Too much espresso in your life?" Pat asked.

"I'm going to need more than espresso if this keeps up all week. All the rooms on the island are booked solid. Don't worry. We've got one of the teens coming in to help. Loved the vid by the way. Lotta has it showing on my laptop up at the counter."

"Vid?" Pat asked, busy putting cream in her cup. The place made the best strong coffee on the island, and Pat's attention was all on anticipating the perfect brew.

"Don't play coy with me. You could have mentioned this event ahead of time as a favor to your friends. Never mind. This is as much business as we care to handle."

"Where's Lotta?" Pat asked, suddenly noticing the owner's absence.

"Oh, she had to go over to the mainland to meet someone in Bayfield. She'll be back tonight."

"I'm going to go look," Deb said. She stood and picked up her cup while walking over to the counter. "Pat! Come look," she called a moment later. "It's us!"

Pat reluctantly got up and went to stand by Deb.

"Oh, that's just that funny little joke thing Martin was going to make, remember? We forgot to ask him if he ever finished it. He must have." She turned to the waitress. "How on earth did you find it?" For Pat, trying to find something specifically on the web, let alone on YouTube, seemed like going into a dark forest without a flashlight.

"Find it?" she laughed. "Besides the fact that it's being linked to the Island Chamber web site, you mean? Everyone's been looking at it."

Just then, two older women walked past them, watching the screen over their shoulders.

"Oh, look, it's the invitation."

They both did a little imitation of the dancing figures on the screen. One of the women did a double take upon seeing Pat and Deb.

"Say, aren't you them?" she asked, pointing to the screen.

Deb blushed.

"Yup, that's us alright. Funny isn't it? One of our kids made it," she explained.

"Well, we're just glad they did. We came from San Francisco because of it." Taking Deb's hand, the woman pumped it vigorously. "It's great to meet you. We already signed up for your 'So You Want to Write' class. Wait until we tell our friends that we met you personally. Well, we won't keep you. See you at solstice." Turning to leave, the woman began humming *Come to the Islands,* the tune from the video.

The woman laughed again.

"Fresh donuts. Any takers? Yours are free today for bringing us so much business."

After eating two donuts each, and paying their bill, they headed out the door.

"You know there are an awful lot of women out here," Deb noted, looking down the street. Pat shook her head dismissively, not bothering to look. She was eager to get their luggage stored at the cabin.

"There must be something else happening this week."

As if to belie her words, a young mom approached her.

"Oh, I'm so glad we're doing this for solstice. What a good model for our daughters," she said, nodding at the little tow headed girl who clung firmly to her hand. "Thanks, ladies."

"Who was that?" Deb wondered as the woman strode purposefully away, the solemn eyes of the little girl looking back.

"Dance, Mommy," she said, her eyes twinkling in recognition.

"Must be someone who lives on the island." As they approached the log cabin, Pat changed the subject. "Here we are, and just like normal, the key is in the door for us. Don't they get the concept of key and lock?" She shook her head.

"This is an island. If someone robs the place, where are they going to go? Do you think it would be easy to get on the ferry with a bunch of stolen vases and not get caught? Relax, most of the planning is done and organized. Now we get to just relax and enjoy."

And with that, Deb pushed open the door on what would be their most challenging adventure to date.

Chapter Seven
June 20

"Oh, oh. There's going to be more to this retreat than I thought," Pat said to herself. While waiting for their friends to arrive, she sat down and picked up an old notebook lying on the side table. Idly glancing through it, she got up, started rummaging through drawers, and pulling out others. She sat back down to study them.

"Hey, look at this, will you?" Pat grunted as she pulled herself up from a trench in the well-used couch. She waved it at Deb who was busy putting on a pot of water to boil for tea.

"Isn't it great to be here at last?" came the response from the kitchen. Coming into the room, she plopped herself down in a big old wooden chair next to Pat.

"Whatcha got?"

Handing her the black journal, Pat pointed to the cover.

"It's the thingy people write in when they rent the cabin. This one only goes back five years. This cabin was built in 1905. Can you believe it? So I looked in a few drawers and guess what I found? Other journals. You're holding the earliest one in your hands."

Avoiding the couch this time, Pat sat down and put her feet up.

"Cool, huh?"

"Look, it starts on June twenty-first, on a solstice." Deb paused a moment trying to read the faded date. "Looks like... 1912."

Pat took an afghan from the back of the couch and covered herself.

Even in June it could be cool out on Madeline. *Glad I brought my long johns,* she thought. Glancing over, she saw that Deb had turned on a floor lamp and was squinting at the writing.

"Read it out loud... Please." She settled in comfortably. She knew Deb would read it since she loved history.

"Let me just figure it out first. It's so faded." Reaching out, Deb grabbed her glasses from the end table.

"There, that's better... hmmm."

Just then a steamy whistling noise came from the other room.

"Stay there," Pat said. Afghan around her shoulders, she headed for the small kitchen. "Do you want passion peach or green?" Already engrossed in deciphering the words, Deb didn't answer.

"Guess its passion peach then." After taking out the cups and saucers and steeping the tea, Pat found a pretty, antique, wooden tray to put them on. *The people who own the cabins are so thoughtful,* she thought, finding honey, napkins and even a tin of cookies to add to her tray. She brought it all back into the living room and handed a cup to Deb, along with two cookies on a napkin.

"So, can you figure it out?" she asked as she took her first sip. *Perfect.*

Deb put her cup down on the floor beside her chair, the tea forgotten for the moment.

"Listen to this."

Adjusting her glasses and holding the book to the light, she haltingly began to read.

Greetings!   21 June 1972

    How nice to be the first guests in your cabin! We've had such fun exploring the island and picknicking on the shore. The boys were even invited to play a game of baseball. They loved it.

    The beach was especially enjoyable for me. We brought along the chairs and table that you so thoughtfully provided. While the boys swam, I sat and watched them, enjoying the sun. I was dozing in its warmth when I was startled awake, by a beautiful woman about my age who offered me some blackberries she had just picked... So I invited her to sit and share a cup of tea. Watching the boys, we exchanged stories. It was as if we had been long-time friends or even sisters. Her little brown dog sat quietly at her side and the wind was balmy, the sun was warm. Time flew by.

    As the boys left the water, she thanked me for the tea, embraced me saying "Welcome to my island." Then she must have walked off with her dog. I didn't see as I was distracted by the boys. Later My husband teased me saying "I didn't see anyone. "Are you sure you weren't dreaming in the sun?" Which I know very well I wasn't since I had the blackberries as proof.

    I'm writing because although I'm sure she told me her name, I can't quite remember it.

I'm hoping you'll know who she is so you can pass on my thanks for the berries.

Thankyou once again for your kind hospitality. We have left the rental fee on the kitchen table as you have asked. See you next summer.

Yours Sincerely,
Mrs Harvey Long

"Isn't that interesting?" Deb asked.

"She must have been one of the year-round folks, the stranger I mean. Welcome to my island indeed," Pat answered as she snuggled farther down into her covers. "Blackberries sound so good."

"Or she could have been from a summer family. You know how they are. Sometimes been here for generations, think they own the place. Anyway," Deb pondered, "don't you wish you knew the rest of the story? Who the strange beautiful woman was? Why she disappeared before the husband and boys could meet her? And..." She stopped after glancing over at her friend and realized by the gentle rise and fall of the afghan, that Pat was fast asleep. Smiling, Deb picked up her cup, took a sip, and went back to reading. She, too, was soon fast asleep.

A knock on the door woke Deb from her unexpected nap.

"Hello!"

Her friend Noreen stepped just inside the cabin, duffle bag in one hand, a large antique easel in the other. Setting her bag on the floor, she ran her fingers through her short-cropped hair. Looking around she sighed with pleasure.

"I haven't been back to this place since the last time we girls got together here. What's it been? Two years?"

"At least. Look at you!" Deb said, as she entered the kitchen. "You've put on weight! You look marvelous, darling."

Noreen beamed.

"I'm up to my pre-chemo weight," she said proudly. "Which room is mine?"

"Use the one you had last time, or pick out another one. Your choice. Except Pat and I have already claimed our old rooms. Creatures of habit, I guess." She hugged her dear friend. Noreen had been in Pat's very first parish, so Pat had met her first, but Deb loved her as if they were sisters.

"Hey, what am I, chopped liver? I'm here, too," called a cheerful voice from the back steps behind Noreen. Deb reached out to hug Julie, who entered carrying a toolbox.

Her dark eyes flashing with excitement, Julie took off her rhinestone embroidered baseball cap and gracefully flung it on the hook by the door.

"And look at you!" Deb marveled. "You look younger every time I see you. You've still got it, girl. You could still be a model," she teased. Hand behind her neck, Julie feigned a pose.

"What's all the ruckus?" asked Pat as she came in with a load of wood from the back yard. "Welcome!" She dropped the wood by the Franklin stove. "Glad you made it early. We could use a good fire starter. It's a bit chilly in here. Did you see the rooms? Of course not, you just got here. Are you taking your same room?" Pat asked, turning to Noreen.

"That's what we were just talking about. I think I'll let Julie pick which one she wants first," Noreen replied graciously.

"I don't care which room I have as long as it has clean sheets and no snoring dog lying on the floor. Whew. I'm just glad I found someone to make breakfast at the B and B so we could get here a little early. It'll be a chance to catch up."

"Hey, we've got a whole four days for that. Isn't it great? You two pick a room then, and I'll break out the tea and cookies. Or would you rather we start with Vodka Slushes?" Pat teased. Whenever they got together it was their drink of choice, a signal that they were on vacation.

"Let's just start with the tea," Julie called as she checked out the first bedroom off the living room. "Ooh, isn't this bench in here adorable?"

"We can make that!" all four women called out at once, laughing at the memories of craft projects they had attempted together in the past.

"Well at least I won't have the store police coming after me for stealing ideas for furniture we want to make on our own," Pat called from the kitchen.

Once, when the women had been shopping she had drawn a picture of a store bench and taken its measurements so they could reproduce it at home. The saleswoman had admonished Pat and asked her to leave. Properly chided, they had never quite gotten around to making the bench.

"You take this one, if you like it," Noreen said to Julie, gesturing towards a room, "and I'll take the one next door. Or do we have to double up?" she continued as she walked back into the front room. "Is anyone else sleeping here?"

"Nope," Deb replied. "There's just enough room for four. Our other friends, Linda, Carolyn and Bev are staying right next door. It's handicapped accessible so Bev can even get her electric cart inside. Linda's already planning to bring some meals in. She's such a good organizer. We'll snack at their place, if that's okay."

"Fine with me," Julie answered as she emerged from the bedroom, having already stuffed her few belonging into the drawers. "As long as I don't have to cook. I get enough of that from working at the family store and the B and B. I'm on vacation!"

"Talk about doubling up," Deb continued as she helped Pat set out a tray of goodies. "We just heard from Sadie at the Lakeside Café that all the rentals on the island have been booked. I wonder if something else is happening right now out here. It would be horrible if there was some male bonding thingy going on at the same time, wouldn't it?"

Noreen and Julie just looked at each other and tried not to laugh.

"We know what it is," Julie said, "but first let's sit down and have our treats. If you really don't know, you might want to put something stronger in your tea. Do you want to break the news to them," she asked, turning to Noreen "or shall I?"

"You tell them about all the women, and I'll tell them about what happened on the ferry, if they're over the shock by then."

"What are you two going on about?" Deb asked, taking a sip of her tea. "Are a group of men really having some kind of meeting out here? Don't worry. I'm sure we can stay out of their way."

"No men. Women. Haven't you seen the YouTube video about this event?"

"Oh, that," Pat said dismissively. "Martin did that as a lark. You know his sense of humor. His wife got the invite, and he couldn't resist being funny. He asked us to just use my iPhone to send him something and so we did. As a matter of fact, when we stopped at Lotta's and picked up these great cookies," She paused and took a big bite of one. "Sadie showed it to us. No big deal."

"So, you really don't know what's been happening?" Julie laughed. "It's become an overnight wonder. In the last week, it's had fifty thousand hits! Everyone in this whole region has seen it, of course, since they know you. And they've been sending it to friends and relatives."

"But that's not all," Noreen added, "it's like the woman singer, Susan Boyle, from Scotland. It's gone viral. I can't believe you don't know this. That's why the rooms are so booked up. Women are coming from everywhere. Our ferry was totally full, and there were people waiting for the next one already." Noreen couldn't hold it in any longer. She leaned back in her chair and laughed. "You are an Internet wonder!"

Pat and Deb just stared at them.

"You're kidding, right? Why would anyone come out here from just watching that silly little video? And what," wailed Pat as she started to realize the ramifications, "will we do with them all?"

"First we'll have another cup of strong black tea," said Deb, pouring everyone some more from the pot, "and then, we'll punt! We'll have to put our heads together after the others arrive."

"If there's another problem, you better lay it on us now," Pat said. "Was there something happening on the ferry? Did the captain ask you to steer?"

"Steer? Are you crazy? The boat was totally full and chaotic. He had enough on his mind besides the two of us running into the shore. No, this one really isn't something you have to fix, thank goodness."

"Well what is it? I'm all ears." Pat leaned forward with her elbows on the table. "Anything to not think about what we're going to do with all those women at tomorrow's breakfast at the church."

"All the ferry workers were in a dither," Noreen said. "That woman who takes your tickets? She hardly even smiled and she gave me back more in change than I gave her in the first place. I handed her back the money, and she had such a blank look on her face, that I asked her if something was wrong. I thought maybe she was sick or something. But no, she said she was fine, and sorry for giving the wrong change. But what with a person missing from the last ferry count, it was like she was in a big funk."

"Missing from the ferry? You mean someone got on and then didn't get off in Bayfield?"

"That's exactly what I asked her. And she said, rather defensively I might add, that she always kept a very accurate count. That she had never been wrong before. Besides, the count of the tickets bore her out. They had never had a person jump from the ferry before, in all the years of its existence."

"Jump? They think someone committed suicide right off the ferry?" Deb asked in dismay.

"That's exactly what I asked her. Then she leaned in and whispered, 'or God forbid, was pushed.' When she realized she was telling me more than she should, her face closed up and got all red, and she said she was sure it was some kind of mistake. Although to tell you the truth, the police were there, so someone was taking it seriously."

There was momentary silence around the table.

"I just hope it was a mistake and some poor woman didn't go overboard into that cold water," Pat said finally. "Your body can go into hypo-thermia in a few minutes even in the bay. The water never warms up on the big lake." Everyone shivered at the thought.

The four women sat sipping tea together in silence for several minutes.

"My grandbaby is cutting his first teeth!" Noreen gushed, lifting the heaviness of the mood.

"My little beastie, Joey, is chewing up furniture!" Pat countered.

"Well, I have you all beat," Deb replied. My granddaughter, Gracie, is only three and she climbs out windows in her bedroom! Now they have to lock them."

Competitive stories about grandchildren were something new for these women since they had all waited to become grandmothers. and each of them loved it.

Their bragging session was interrupted by a loud tapping on the back door.

"Knock, knock. Is this an open party?" a light-hearted voice hooted. "Did we come to the right place?"

"Hi Carolyn! Come on in!" Pat's voice sang out.

A middle-aged woman, her wispy hair helmeting her face, bustled into the room.

"Wow! You really got us a good deal on this place," Carolyn said, look-ing admiringly around the room.

She was followed closely by a petite blonde, dressed impeccably in a blue and white nautical polo and khaki capris.

"Hi, Linda. Good to see you," Deb said, standing to hug Linda.

There's nothing like a friend you raised your babies with, Deb thought.

Deb pulled up more chairs to the table.

"You know each other, right?" They all nodded.

The women settled into family gossip, as women do when they get together, as they relaxed slowly into island time.

"Okay, enough small talk," Carolyn said. "What do you want us to do for the retreat?"

"I really don't know," Pat said. "We thought we were all organized. Free breakfast on me to anyone who comes up with a plan to deal with all the extra women."

"We're so glad you invited us. Why did you decide to have this retreat, anyway?" Linda asked, turning to Deb.

"Because we're still crazy after all these years, I guess," Deb joked. "Seriously, though, we had been thinking about those times when we got together years ago when our kids were little. Remember how we were crazy young single parents back then and how good it felt to get away for a weekend? Remember the freedom we felt to do whatever we wanted?"

"Those were the days," Carolyn said. "Remember how Linda made us all get up to watch the sunrise over Lake Superior?"

"I remember laughter, escape, and growing," Deb said. "And not around the belly, either. Seems to me we were all pretty svelte back then."

"And at least two of you still are," Julie chimed in.

"Anyway, we wanted to try to create a renewed sense of community by gathering women at solstice... doing things we love to do... trying to feel a little younger... maybe take a few risks in our thinking."

They put their heads together and brainstormed for the next half an hour – where the writing workshop should be; how to set up for extras at the painting class; and where they would feed everyone.

"Jeeze, I gotta stop," Deb said suddenly. "I thought this was just going to be a great weekend for fun." She stood up and rubbed her lower back with her hands. "I need to just lie down and think. I need a time out. I'm going in my room for while."

"Go ahead Deb. We'll just finish up deciding where everything's going to take place. Don't worry," Pat said.

Settling into the comforter on the bed, Deb kept thinking about the dream she and Pat had envisioned. It was so simple: friends coming, good food, and laughter. Whatever happened to that idea anyway?

"What about bathrooms?" Deb heard Linda ask from the next room.

Damn! The weekend the stranger went missing from the ferry! And how could she be missing anyway? There were so many people on the boat. Truth is, Deb thought, *they probably wouldn't have noticed. People go through life as if it's a dream and purposely don't notice anything that might cause them to wake up and look around. Well; I'm not going to sleep through life!*

And with that last thought she promptly fell asleep.

Chapter Eight
June 20

Deb's rest was shortlived. Just as she settled into her nap, she heard the island tune of her cell singing faintly from another part of the cabin. She awoke with a small snort and reached for it on the night stand. It wasn't there.

"Snap! Where is that crazy thing? Anyone see my cell out there?" she called. "Sometimes I swear it has legs and just waits for me to turn the other way so it can run and hide."

Having gotten up to follow the sound, Pat handed Deb the ringing phone as she came out of the bedroom.

"Here it is. It was in a white Macy's bag on the sofa."

"Bag? See what I mean?" Deb said. It stopped ringing just as she opened the lid. She sighed. "Missed that one. Oh well. Oh, look there's three more messages I missed."

Putting her feet up on Noreen's chair rung, Deb squinted at the small symbols and pressed the button she hoped would bring up messages. For some reason known only to the mysterious phone gods, the setting was on speaker phone.

"Hello, Deb. Pick up if you're there. This is St. John's. Are you on the island yet? Call me as soon as you can. I've got my secretary calling in food for the breakfast feast, and we'll open the weaving room to set up more seating. We're on top of it, although we probably could use a few more dish-washers. Oh, and dishes. The church only has settings for one-fifty. Never mind, but call me with the crowd number. There are other things to decide. Bye for now. Call me." Click.

She pressed the button again, while the others listened curiously.

Beep. "Hi, Deb. I tried to get Pat, but it seems her phone is off. The sign-up sheets we put up for the workshops are almost all full. Should we start making second sessions for all of them? Need to know ASAP. Oh, and we have permission to close off Bell Street for Tai Chi in the mornings. You're very welcome. It doesn't hurt to be one of the only police officers on the island. Call me." Click.

Beep. "Hi, Mom. This is Cliffy. Are you picking me up from school? Call me." Click.

"That kid! He knows I'm gone." She pressed the button again.

Beep. "Hi, my darling. I tried calling Patty but she never answers. What kind of a person has a phone if they never bother to answer it, anyway? Would you tell her your Mom and I are on our way? We'll be on the 8:30 ferry tonight. No need to pick us up. See you at your cabin." There was a pause. "Oh yes... this is Jessie. Call me. Bye." Click.

Just as she closed her phone and was about to put it down on the table, it rang again.

"Hello? This is Deb."

"Deb, glad I caught you. Say, now that there's so gosh awful many coming, is it okay if we have two specials and then when they're out we can have people order off the menu? The discount will still apply. We didn't really plan for this kind of crowd."

"Lotta, is that you? Are you talking about lunch tomorrow? You think it will be that crowded?"

"Well, we have one hundred reservations already. Say, did you happen to reserve a table? We're a popular place, you know. Just kidding. We've reserved a head table for you and yours at noon."

"That would be great, thanks," Deb replied. "I just can't believe this yet. Thanks for the heads up, Lotta. Bye."

"Is that a coupon special?" Carolyn asked. "Do I need a coupon?"

Deb sat silently for a moment.

Pat looked at her friend and was concerned by her pallor. "Are you okay?"

"Okay? If by okay you mean crazy nuts, then I'm okay. This is another fine mess you've got me in, Ollie," she joked, holding her head in her hands.

"We'll figure this out," Pat replied, patting her back. She was about to say more when there was another knock on the door.

"What now?" Pat rose from the table and opened the door to five women she had never met before in her life.

"Halloo, is this where we register for the solstice, or is there a tent somewhere to sign in?" the voice floated.

Deb's groan could be heard all the way from the kitchen.

"Is someone ill?" the voice asked politely.

"If only I were," replied the voice as if through a brain fog.

"I'm going to work on a master schedule until it's time to meet Bev in Bayfield," Deb said, turning to the others.

"I'll go check on how many people can fit on the beach," Linda offered.

"C'mon, Noreen," Julie said. "Let's go see where your class is going to be held."

While engrossed in her scheduling project Deb noticed her cell phone buzzing with a signal of another unheard message.

Jeeze, didn't I turn the ringer off? she thought.

Beep. "Hi, Deb. It's Mike, from the ferry line. Just wanted to let you know that my wife would like to join you for part of the retreat tomorrow." The voice hesitated.

"And you probably heard already, but I thought I would give you a heads up. There seems to be a woman missing off the ferry from the morning trek right after yours. It serves me right to brag about my record. I'll catch you later. Bye. Call me." Click.

So someone really is missing. It's probably not as bad as I think, Deb reassured herself. *Don't go making a big deal about this. You've got enough to do.*

She picked up her pen and paper and added Mike's wife to the list.

She returned all her phone calls and made an even bigger list, trying to distract her mind from her creeping anxiety. Having finished all that she could for the moment, and taking a deep breath, she glanced at the clock in the corner.

Having no more chores to do before it was time to leave for the ferry, she picked up another journal from a pile on the shelf in the corner. She paged through it slowly, enjoying the messages of past guests. One in particular caught her eye.

July 6 1985

Hello? My Mom said I could write here. This is my first letter. do I put the date in like she said. Today we leave the island. I DONT WANT to go!! I had the most fun in my whole life here. which is funny because I didnt want to come, but My Mom made me. She said I would like it and she was ~~right~~ right! [I wish mom wasnt always right.

I met a girl on the beach. She was 10 like me and has a puppy! He was so cute!! I got to help her teach it to swim. Then he chased sticks and even rocks in the water.

I asked her if she would be my forever friend. ~~Xxxxx~~ I have never had one before, but I really need one now. My Mom and I are moving to Boston and I wont know anyone there. The girl said she would never forget me and when I come Back she would be here. She is so lucky to live here. I wish I was her. ♥ Katelyn

Deb smiled, remembering herself at age ten in those long ago days of summer innocence.

How I wish that Pat and I had known each other as little girls.

"C'mon, Deb, time to go, or we'll miss the ferry," Pat's voice called.

"Coming!" Deb replied, placing the book tenderly back on the shelf.

"Anything we can do while you're gone to help get ready?" Julie asked cheerfully from her perch in the rocker.

"Let me think. We need to make sure we have enough garbage cans," Pat replied as she grabbed her jacket from the hook. "You can call the Bell Street Tavern to ask for more. We need to make sure there are enough toilets available to accommodate all the people. Linda, you were right. You could call some of the Main Street businesses and see if they will act as a D.T."

"What's a D.T?" asked Noreen.

"A designated toilet, of course," Pat replied.

"Oh, and one more thing," she continued, as she opened the door to the cabin.

"What's that?" Julie asked. "Lay it on me your highness."

"Pray for a miracle."

"A solstice miracle," Deb added over her shoulder as she closed the door behind them.

Chapter Nine
June 20

Forty minutes later, Pat sat once again on the bench by the Bayfield dock, waiting for Bev to arrive. As she waited she indulged in her favorite hobby of people watching. There were people bringing wagons of fresh veggies for restaurants, a couple with bicycles, and a cute little baby boy squirming in his mother's arms. All of them were hurrying to get on the ferry before it left.

Just think, Pat daydreamed. *In a few days, I'll be holding my own little squirming JoJo.*

A noise startled her out of her grandmotherly thoughts. Driving right past all the other cars waiting in line, her least favorite policeman brought his squad car to a screeching halt. Red-faced, he turned to the pretty woman sitting next to him. Even from a distance Pat could see that he was yelling as he stopped the car. The woman opened the door, pulled out a small suitcase and slammed it shut. Spying a free space on the bench, she sat down. He glared at the two of them sitting together and sped off.

"Damn. I forgot my sunglasses in the car. Look at him go," she said shaking her head. "Don't you think he should get a ticket for tearing out of a public lot like that?" she asked, without looking up.

"I don't think he would give himself a ticket," Pat ventured. "Though he's given one to just about everyone else in the area."

"Don't I know it? He's given me three, and I'm his wife!"

"Oops, sorry."

"Believe it, not half as sorry as he's going to be."

Glancing at Pat for the first time, a look of recognition registered in the woman's eyes.

"Don't I know you?"

"I seem to be getting a lot of that lately."

"Anyway, I'm going out for the retreat. I took off from work and I'm coming all three days."

"Well, good for you. I'm just waiting for a friend who has to get her scooter on the ferry. She probably doesn't need the help, but she might appreciate me clearing pathways for her."

"Oh her? I saw her with a redhead over in the parking lot as we came through. I hope my husband doesn't give her a ticket," the woman grumbled. Catching Pat's eye, they laughed.

"Husbands!" they both said at exactly the same time. Smiling, Pat waved at Deb and Bev coming towards them. The red scooter was making a path through the crowd.

"What are you waiting for? I've got Tarot cards to read!" Bev called out excitedly. "Thanks for meeting me, but I could have handled it."

Pat stood up and gave Bev a big hug.

"I know, but I couldn't wait. It's so good to see you." Greetings over, the three friends made their way toward the ferry as the policeman's wife followed them.

Soon, they sat gabbing in the shelter of the small porch of the ferry with legs stretched out in front of them.

"I just got back from San Antonio last week," Bev chirped happily. How are your kids doing in Houston? I thought of going to see them while I was down there but just didn't make it happen."

The women's gaiety was interrupted just then by a banging of the red metal door. Captain Mike entered the small space. Deb looked up and smiled.

"Hi, Mike. How are you doing?"

Mike just stared at her silently.

"Mike, I'd like you to meet an old friend of mine. This is Beverly from Minneapolis. Bev, this is Mike, the captain of this ferry."

"Nice to meet you," Bev said sweetly, offering her hand in greeting. "But how on earth are we moving without the Captain steering this boat?" she puzzled aloud.

"I left my assistant at the helm."

Mike's shoulders were slumped and there was a deep furrow in his brow.

"Hey, Mike, is everything taken care of?" Deb asked. "I got your message just before we came. Did it all work out?"

"Well... no," he started slowly. "It's just that our counts didn't match after we arrived back at the Bayfield dock."

"What counts do you mean?" Deb asked.

"We always keep tabs on the cars and people. We try to head off any attempts to cheat the system with stowaways.

"Jeez, I had no idea you did that for every single trip. It must be a lot of work keeping track of everyone."

"Sure is. But it's got to be done," Mike replied. "So, wouldn't you know it? Right after I was bragging about my perfect record this morning, we ended up missing someone on the trip right after yours. And I don't know who it is," he continued. "I asked the ticket taker if maybe she had miscounted. 'Oh, no,' she said, 'I am very careful.' And she is. Her numbers matched mine, so that lessens the likelihood of a mistake."

"So what do you think it means?" Deb inquired attentively, her attention piqued by Mike's serious tone.

"I have my hunches, but I just can't be sure at this point. The simplest explanation is that someone just hitched a ride in someone else's car and wasn't seen leaving by my employees."

Pat and Bev listened silently with wide eyes.

"Marc always says that the simplest explanation is usually the most likely. That's how he approaches medical diagnoses anyway," Deb agreed.

"I want to be optimistic about this," Mike answered, "but if someone fell or was pushed overboard, we are quickly losing our window for rescue in these cold waters. Even a strong swimmer can't last long in waves like these. We had to call the Coast Guard," he said glumly. "That was humbling."

"Do you really think someone went overboard?" Pat asked.

"Here's what troubles me. One of the other passengers approached me and told me something as we were verifying our counts at the dock."

"What was that?" Deb pried.

"The guy is a year round islander. He knows everyone and can tell locals from tourists. He went gaga over a woman while he was waiting at the dock. She was about sixty, with gorgeous hair. He joined her on the bench and they talked about the weather while they waited.

He's been a widower for a number of years and it's been awhile since he has been in the company of a good woman. Poor guy. I could tell by the gleam in his eye that he really liked that one."

"How old is he?" Deb inquired.

"Oh, he retired a few years ago, so he must be in his late sixties. But he's still sharp as a tack and a man of his word. If he says something is so, then it is," Mike said with assurance.

"Anyway, the story he told me is that he lost the woman in the crowd as he started off the ferry. He saw her disappear between the cars. He was following her, hoping to get her phone number. He searched upstairs and down afterwards and found no sign of her. He assumed that she had somehow snuck past him and gotten off the boat without him seeing her and had chalked it up to just another day of striking out. Then he overheard me and the ticket taker talking about our counts not matching."

"Wow," Deb and Pat said at once, slowly putting together the pieces.

"Do you think someone really disappeared? Could it have been that woman?" Deb wondered aloud.

"I think it was just a coincidence," Pat asserted. "With all the crowds today, there were just way too many people to keep track of."

"I wish we could help you sort this out, Mike," Deb replied sympathetically. "Sorry, we have bigger fish to fry right now, like how we're going to feed and house all these people we weren't expecting. But, where do you go from here, Mike?"

"Well, I have to investigate this more. As much as I hate to do it, I will need to file a report on the discrepancy. The problem is, I can't spare the staff to go talk to people. We are just too damn busy with all these women coming here today. I'm already paying overtime the way it is. They keep coming in waves. You'd think it was July fourth or something!"

"What did the Coast Guard say?" Deb asked, feeling somewhat responsible for his predicament due to the large crowds coming to the retreat.

"The last I heard they haven't found a thing."

"Are they doing a search and rescue?" Pat asked.

"Not officially. They sent one boat to look around. The problem is, no one saw anyone go over and there's no real description of a person, so it's hard to even know where to look."

"What can we do to help?" Deb blurted out.

Oops, she thought. *Once again, my lips move in response to a situation I can't control.* If there had been a table on the boat, Pat would have kicked Deb's leg under it. Instead, she gave Deb a reproachful look.

"I know you're busy," Mike said gratefully. "Here's what you can do. You two women seem to notice things that others don't. Make me a list of people to talk to. Maybe you can ask around and see if anyone else noticed anything the least bit unusual or noticed the woman. See what you can find out. I'd really appreciate it."

"I'm doing Tarot readings with the group," Bev volunteered. "I can ask around."

"We'll put our heads together and see what we can come up with," Deb offered helpfully.

"But we're not getting involved with any kind of investigation," Pat reminded.

"Thanks, ladies," Mike replied with relief. "Here's my card with my cell number. Let me know what you find out. Call me." Then he turned and walked out the door.

Deb's mind was whirling as she turned back to Pat and Bev, who sat in thoughtful silence.

Pat was the first to break the quiet.

"What have you gone and done this time, girlfriend?" she asked with a hint of worry in her voice. "We really don't have time for this right now, you know."

"How on earth can anyone get lost on a ferry?" Deb replied, ignoring Pat. "It's only about the size of my house. Come to think of it, lots of things get lost in my house, but never any people, so far, anyway!"

"I suppose the woman could have jumped over," offered Bev.

"Suicide? But the way the guy described her to Mike, it sounds like she was happy and serene," Pat argued begrudgingly. "I don't think that's highly likely."

"What if someone pushed her?" Deb said.

"On purpose, you mean? Come on, Deb. You're a little jaded from coming across those two bodies in the last few years," Pat retorted. "Besides, it was late morning on a bright, sunny day. And with all those people on board, don't you think someone would have heard a splash? I would have heard a splash, wouldn't you?"

"No. But with all the motor noise and excitement, even if I had heard one I wouldn't have thought anything of it," Deb said.

"No matter what you want to believe, people find all sorts of reasons to end their lives or at the very least to appear to disappear," Bev said sagely.

"As far as I know, it's never happened here, though," Pat replied.

"What if she was trying to escape from an abusive relationship, or running from the I.R.S., or grieving the loss of a beloved boyfriend?" Bev continued.

"Or pretending to disappear so that her mother can't call her?" Deb joked. "Just kidding, you know," she added quickly.

"Well, all kidding aside, I think it was just a mistake in counting," Pat said. "With all those people, surely they could have missed one somewhere. I don't think we should let our imaginations run wild, like the characters in Evanovich novels. Remember, Deb, getting sucked into solving a mystery isn't that much fun, as we both well know." She gave Deb a knowing smile and Deb reached over and patted her arm.

Deb pressed her face to the window, now facing west up the channel between the Apostle Islands. The sun shone on the water as through a prism, reflected in dancing droplets of light that sparkled on the crystal clear inland sea. Her concern momentarily vanished; Deb's awareness was blissfully drawn to watching the reflected light on the water.

Little did she know that they would all soon be embroiled in the case of a missing woman.

Chapter Ten
June 20

Taking advantage of the quiet cabin while Deb and Pat were away meeting Bev, Linda used her spare time to settle in. Opening the closet in her room, she reached in to hang her clothes and line her things up in the empty space.

Pushing the hung clothes over to the left to make more room, she noticed a shelf piled with black leather books, stacked neatly in the far corner. Curiosity got the better of her. Reaching in and taking out the book on top, she brushed off a layer of dust with her finger and wiped her hands off on her pants.

Island Memories was embossed in gold on the front cover.

Oh, my gosh, what on earth is this? she wondered.

Opening the book and sitting down in a comfy chair, she paged through the handwritten entries and started to read.

> June 30 1945
> Thank you!
> We spent a lovely weekend on the island. We played croquet many times and enjoyed your well-tended walking trails. You would never know there was a war going on while in this tranquill place. On Saturday while he was out fishing, I sat in your beautiful Tea House, enjoying the birdsong and the smell of cedar.

"My husband is a good man. Hardworking, kind, and stable. Except he went and reupped without talking to me first. How like a man! Now he's down in Florida, working as a navy mechanic, leaving me to tend two teenagers. The truth is we don't have fun anymore. I wanted to dance and he wanted to go for Sunday drives, to the same places, on the same ROADS. Over and over and _over_!

I wanted to entertain and have parties. He wanted to sit and listen to the radio. I was so angry and embarrassed about having an old husband in the service. And then he was gone.

Then came Joe, the happy Irishman with the smiling eyes, who waltzed into my life one day when I was out on the town with the girls after work. He took me by the hand WITH a wink and a twirl around the dance floor, like I've never been twirled before. My life has been a whirlwind ever since.

We had so much fun together. I feel so young, so hopeful, and so carefree. Is that a sin?

My future is not set. I have to decide. I really don't want to hurt my family, but I'm not getting any younger.

While I was sitting, a delightful young woman brought me out a pot of tea. When I first noticed her walking I was struck by her hair, it was kissed with sunshine. She was a wisp of a girl, dressed in a tailored dress and sandals. Deeply tanned, she was about my age. A large tawny colored dog walked placidly at her side. So personable and friendly that I just knew I could trust her. So I
asked her to sit a minute. Soon we were into a long

asked her to sit a minute. Pouring water into a bowl she set it by her feet for her companion. Chatting away we passed the time, and I talked about things I've not shared with anyone. And here I am doing it again. It must be the island.

I told her about my life, and she counseled me to write it all down. That it might help.

I wonder, isn't there more to life than duty and responsibility? My parents see my husband is a perfect match, but he's so old. Twelve years older to be exact.

"My God! They have the same age difference as my husband and I do!" Linda said out loud. She continued to read.

The woman listened patiently to me and then she turned with a dazzling smile that lit up the gazebo. Go with your passion she said just like that. It will never fail you. I wanted to write that down so I could remember it. At that moment a cardinal sang, as if agreeing with her.

I stopped later at the kitchen to thank her for her kindness, but when I asked for the nice woman who'd brought me tea, I was told, there was no one fitting that description at Coole Park.

I hope someone will pass on my thanks. Honestly, it does feel good to write all this, even if no one ever reads it.
Now back to the mainland, the horn is honking.   Hope to come back

Appreciatively,
Irene, Minneapolis, Minnesota

Linda teared up as she finished.

What's this all about? she wondered. *My own marriage? This could have been me.*

Startled from self-reflection, she turned and looked over her shoulder as the door behind her opened unexpectedly.

"What are you doing in there, friend?" Carolyn asked. "I've been waiting to walk down to the dock with you!"

"Not your business!" Linda snapped.

"Jeeze, Louise, Linda. What's wrong with you?"

"Oh, I am so sorry," she said when she saw Carolyn back up a little. "It's just that I was reading something in an old journal from this cabin and it just upset me."

"What do you mean?"

"This couple stayed here back in 1945 during the war. They weren't even married and the woman's husband was away doing his duty with the Navy. And she was writing about leaving him for her young boyfriend! I just don't understand how anyone would do such a thing."

"We all have our choices in life," Carolyn responded gently, sitting on the bed beside her.

"We sure do."

"Think about it, Linda. Your first husband came back from Vietnam and became a crazy person and you didn't know what to do."

"Don't remind me."

"My point is that we can't always judge the trials of others."

Linda sighed heavily.

"Give me a little time. I just don't feel like going for a walk right now."

"Let me have a look at these. I just love history!" Carolyn reached onto the shelf and pulled out a volume. "Oh, these look like fun, Linda."

Her walk to the dock temporarily forgotten she sat in the rocker, paging through the book. She stopped abruptly in the middle.

"Look! Here's an entry from people named Lundgren from 1906. I have to read this! That was my maiden name you know, Linda."

Linda didn't answer. Her thoughts were far away.

Not noticing Linda's distance, Carolyn began to read aloud.

From the Lundgrens
October 4, 1906

Thank you for making our honeymoon so comfortable and relaxing. We never thought we could have one. My husband is a farmer and we are just starting out. But our dear neighbors in our little town of Brahm, MN insisted that we get away from the homestead before the long winter.

"After all," they said, "the winters are hard up here in this forlorn place and your mid-wiving will keep you from leaving before spring. There's so many young ones waiting to be delivered in the mid-winter and we want you to be rested." So they pooled their money and offered to feed the animals while we are gone so that we could get away.

It took us four days by wagon to get to Bayfield. We left our horses at a stable on the mainland and booked passage on the Chequamegon. Once we arrived on the Island, we hailed a wagon to bring us to this Eden in the woods.

It is like a castle to us. Here, there is running water and flush toilets. I even took some Lux detergent and filled the tub and had myself a bubble bath. Such luxury! I feel like a

Carolyn paused as she thought of her daily dip in her double Jacuzzi. She continued to read.

pampered queen. The food is delicious here, but the companionship even better.

One day last week, I was walking in the woods while my sweetheart was in the fish shack helping filet the catch for dinner.

An adorable golden dog with curly ears came limping up to me and whimpered at my feet, followed closely by a young slim woman with a long pinned-up braid and a bright smile. The woman appeared to be just barely out of her teens.

I knelt down and picked up the pup, who just looked deeply at me with the most mournful brown eyes. She offered me her right front paw and I held it in my hands for a moment while pulling out a thorn. The puppy began to wag her tail and then she licked my face with such vigor that I thought she would take my skin off.

"Oh, you must be a healer," the woman said. "My dog has responded to your touch. Are you a vet?"

"Heavens, no, not a vet. I'm a mid-wife. But I can do paws."

The woman tucked her loose hair into her long braid.

"Bless you," she said. "You make a difference. You have more than most people will ever have in material things. And thank you for your help for my friend here.

She waved and walked into the cabin next door. At that moment a warm breeze blew through the woods rustling my hair and the leaves on the trees. When I remember my meeting with that woman and her dog I can still feel that warm breeze on my face. It was almost the highlight of my time here. I feel so refreshed and ready to return to the busy life on the farm.

I've never thought we had much. But when that woman told

me that, I realized that there is
more to life than a pretty dress
from the Dry Goods Store.

I know we probably won't
return here because a farmer
can't take trips like this. This
has been a trip of a lifetime.
The best part was being reminded
that my life really matters.

We thank you kindly for your
hospitality and all the creature
comforts you provided. Our
wooden wagon seat will feel
lighter as we make our
journey home. We're eager to
get home as we are expecting
a visit from my husband's
brother, Jake, from Omaha.
And I have babies to deliver

Most sincerely yours,
Mrs. Emily Lundgren.

Carolyn gasped.

"Oh my Lord! My great grandfather was from Omaha! These people could be my relatives! But what in the world?" she wondered aloud. "How on earth could anyone live without running water or flushes and still be grateful?

Carolyn's brow furrowed deeply at the thought.

"Surely times have changed. No one could live like that anymore."

"Are you planning a party in here?"

Bev knocked on the door with one hand while hanging onto her walker with the other. Linda stood up.

"Hi, Bev," she said, wrapping her in a tight embrace.

"We didn't even hear you come in," Carolyn said, "but we discovered a treasure trove of history in the closet. And believe it or not, I might just have found one of my few relatives."

"Really?" Bev asked, with interest. "Let me see." She held out her hand.

"Well the name fits, but what are the odds that a relative of mine could show up in a journal entry from 1906 that I just happen to come across?"

"About as likely that you would meet your high school classmate from Omaha on the streets of Bayfield, Wisconsin, during the Apple Fest in a crowd of fifty thousand people," Bev reminded her, looking up from the book.

"You know what Deb always says about Lake Superior. That it's a connector that brings people together."

"If you ask me, this is downright spooky. I wonder what happened to these people after they left this place." Carolyn mused. "I'm going to look this woman up on my iPad and see if I can find out more. Let's just hope they were able to move out of their poor lives and prosper from all their hard work."

"That's not what would make her happy, Carolyn," Bev advised.

Feeling uneasy, Carolyn pulled out her cell phone and dialed hurriedly.

"Hello, honey. Is that you?" she said in a loud voice. "It's me. How's the Bayfield Inn? Is it comfortable enough for you?"

"He's staying in Bayfield?" Bev whispered. "Can't he even let you go away for one weekend?"

"Are you finding enough to do?" Carolyn continued. She paused, listening. "Don't worry. I'll be back soon. Listen. Do you remember where we can get discount coupons for dinner at the Bell Street? I think we might go there to eat tonight. Really? Not during peak season? Is that right? Okay, I just thought I'd check before spending all that money if I don't need to. Love you. Bye. "

Bev raised her eyebrow at Carolyn. Carolyn's coupon cutting was legendary among the women. This time, Carolyn wasn't calling for the coupons.

"Weren't we supposed to be meeting next door?" Linda asked, quietly leaving the room. "I'm going to go see if the coffee's on."

"Let's go check out the town, Noreen," Julie said. "Maybe we can find some places for the extra workshops."

"Extra workshops?" Deb asked.

"Sure, with all the people we'll probably have to add some."

"Yeah, let's go look. Do you want us to ask about available space if we see some likely spots?" Noreen asked as she turned to Pat.

"Sure, that would be great."

"We need a walk and I want to check out my spot for the painting class anyway."

"If you're doing that," Bev said, pushing away from the table and looking at Linda, "let's go and talk to Lotta, the owner of the coffee shop. I've got to put up my signup list for readings." She held up the paper she had been working on.

The four women left the cabin chatting.

"Darn, I could have taught a quilting class if I'd known. Maybe next year," Carolyn said.

"Actually, there is somewhere they might need your expert help. St. John's church has a community store for weavers, potters and quilters who live here on the island," Pat suggested. "You might want to check it out."

"Great idea!"

After Carolyn left, the cabin was suddenly quiet.

"Let's take a cup out on the stoop," Pat said.

"Yes, let's," Deb agreed.

They sat outside the cabin drinking cups of coffee with a little brandy in them to help keep warm.

"Look at all those women coming off the ferry!" Pat said, waving back as a group of native women strolled by chatting and smiling. Rubbing her right knee, Pat started to get up. Deb took her eyes off the wave of people to look at her friend.

"Where are you going? You haven't finished your cup yet, and this may be our only break until the end of the retreat. I made it just the way you like it, with something special added for relaxing."

"I notice you've been doing that a lot lately."

Must be menopausal, Pat thought. Whatever it was, she liked the additive.

"I'll be right back." Without explanation, Pat went through the old screen door, and Deb heard her rummaging around in the kitchen. After a final bang of a cupboard door, Deb started to get up.

What the heck is she doing now? Then smiling, she sat down again as her friend came out with a plate of cookies.

"This may help. They're chocolate chip."

"What we need is not chocolate. What we need is a miracle," Deb said, holding out her hand for a cookie.

"It's probably not as bad as it looks," Pat said. "Probably everyone had the same idea to get here early. Next ferry will probably be *empty.*"

Deb just looked at her. "That's a lot of probablys." She looked up to see a familiar figure coming down the street.

"Is there one more cup for me?" the woman asked, approaching the steps. "Wow! Look at these crowds. It'll be something if they all come to breakfast at the church. We've already bought up all the eggs and bacon at the Island Store."

Pat jumped up and went into the kitchen to get another mug.

"Do you want a booster in it?" she yelled out the door.

"I'm not a drinker myself, but today, sure." Taking a deep sip as Pat handed her the coffee, she put her feet up.

"Do you think you can get more food over on the first ferry?" Pat asked.

"All things are possible with God's help," she replied.

"God and Mike that is," Pat added. The three women spent a few minutes in silence watching the crowds pile off the ferry.

More food? Pat thought. Is this woman crazy? These people can't all be coming for the retreat. It's just not possible!

Good drink, Deb thought, taking another swig from her mug. Almost worth all this bother.

With all the cash we make from the breakfast tomorrow, we will really be able to upgrade the church organ, the island pastor thought.

As the women sat in the twilight, two moving silhouettes approached the cabin.

"I think the clearing in front of Bell Street will work just fine for Pie Chi," Noreen said.

"What about your art class?" Julie asked. "Didn't we say it would work well to have it on the lawn outside the library?"

"Remember, I need to be next to the lake for that. I'd rather take the nearest beach area."

"Oh, hi girls," Deb called. "Did you walk a long way?"

"All the way to the Marina and back," Julie replied. "Don't worry, we have it all figured out."

"That's wonderful," Pat said. "Do you think we have room for everything?"

Julie reached into her pocket and pulled out a map she had retrieved from the Ferry Landing. On it, she had highlighted and labeled a spot for each workshop.

"Looks like you are in good shape," the pastor marveled, standing up. "I see that things are under control. Well, I've got to get back to the church to meet with my breakfast coordinator. She doesn't have a key."

"See you in the morning," Pat said.

"Bye." Waving to them, she walked into the darkness toward the church. "Thanks for the fortification," she added, glancing back over her shoulder.

Julie and Noreen sat for awhile on the steps enjoying the unveiling of the evening sky and pointing out constellations.

Deb's head began to nod from the effects of the brandy. She was roused by the sound of her phone once again breaking into her revelry.

"Hi, it's me," Marc said. "Is everything okay over there? I just saw something on television about a missing woman."

"Television? Really?" Deb's eyes widened.

"Television?" echoed the voices of the others.

Chapter Eleven
June 20

After what seemed like an eternity practicing crisis management and finding spaces for women where there were none, Pat put down her pen and sighed.

"There. No one will sleep out under the stars tonight unless they want to. Let's call it a day."

"I'll pour," Carolyn said, bringing in a tray laden with a pitcher of frozen Vodka Shushes and tall glasses.

"Look! It's our vacation drink. I can't believe we're drinking again," Deb said. "Just one for me. We have a long day tomorrow. Here's to old friends!"

Sitting in the rocker, Bev handed matches to Julie, who was busying herself building a fire in the old woodstove in the corner. Noreen rifled through an antique LP record collection in the corner, looking for suitable music.

"Does anyone have any Tylenol?" Deb asked, rubbing her temples, as she lay on the opposite end of the couch from Pat.

"I do!" Linda replied solicitously. She paused from sweeping up a pile of crumbs and put her broom in the corner.

"What's the matter? Are you not feeling well?"

"I'm worried about how we're going to manage all the crowds tomorrow. I feel like I'm swimming without a life jacket in deep water and about to go under. Whose idea was this, anyway?" she whined, directing her gaze accusingly in Pat's direction.

"It seems to me someone in this room talked about 'building it so they would come.' Didn't know you were such a good carpenter, Deb," Pat retorted.

"Well, I have the hard muscles tonight to prove it," Deb replied, continuing to rub the back of her neck. "Especially in my neck and shoulders. Man, am I tight."

"I heard that there will be hot rock massage on the screen porch at Lotta's tomorrow," Linda offered.

"I'm going to have to get one," Deb replied.

"Lotta's is even serving fancy hors d'oeuvres. I'm sure you could get in," Pat added soothingly. "Anyway, it doesn't matter now. We've done all we can planning this retreat. So, let's talk about the woman who went missing."

"You two aren't feeling responsible for that, are you?" Julie asked, looking over at them and pausing from her fire making. "You know it wasn't your fault."

"Easy to say, but harder to believe," Deb replied. "If we hadn't created so much chaos with all the women on the ferry, maybe the staff could have kept better track of things."

"There you go again, Deb," Pat admonished gently. "Taking responsibility for everything that happens in life. This is not about you. And you don't have to fix it either."

"Did you hear that?" Linda asked suddenly.

"What?" Pat replied.

"It sounds like a scratching noise. Listen."

The women fell silent and strained to hear.

"I thought I heard it," Bev replied. "Maybe I'll get to see my first bear in the wild. I was hoping for that as a matter of fact."

"Maybe it's a porcupine under the porch," Pat said.

"Maybe it's the ghost of that missing woman coming back to haunt us," Noreen teased.

"Get out of here!" Deb replied. "I'm going outside to look. Where's the flashlight?"

"I couldn't find any earlier," Carolyn replied, "but I found candles."

Reaching to the mantle she pulled off a box of white tapers and began handing them around to the other women.

Julie reached into the budding fire in the woodstove and lit her candle, reaching out with a light.

"Silent Night, anyone?" she joked.

"Beats going out there in the dark," Deb answered, lighting her candle first and turning to light the others in turn.

"This is like some bad Gothic novel," Pat remarked. "Five women carrying lit candles into the dark. I know there's a sermon here somewhere."

Leading the way, Deb unlocked the front door opening to the yard. They paused for a moment and listened to the silence. A door slammed behind them, causing them to jump.

It was a clear starlit night. Deb could hear a crunching noise to the left side of the cabin.

She walked stealthily in the dark toward the sound, practicing the soft step learned from her walking meditation in Yoga class. The other women huddled together on the steps.

"It sounds like someone is whacking the ground with a stick," Deb whispered.

Ahead of her lurked a large shadowy shape on the ground. She could just make out an outline.

"What the heck. It almost looks human. Is someone hurt?" she asked. The dark shadow moved up and down as if it was breathing. She took a deep breath, summoning her courage as she took a step closer to the form. One step, followed by a pause, and then another. The dark shape moved at the sight of the light.

Crunch... crunch... crunch...

"Hello!" Deb called softly. "Do you need help?"

"I'm going back in," Carolyn said in the darkness behind Deb. "I'm calling the police."

"Shh! I doubt there's any police on duty out here now at this hour. We're on an island, for heaven's sake!" Pat whispered. She walked quietly behind Deb.

Deb crept slowly toward the noise, holding her candle boldly upright toward the night sky. Ahead of her she could see two glowing eyes low to the ground reflected in the light.

"I can't stand this," Pat said in a shaky voice. "The last time I saw eyes like that it was a skunk in my path on the way to the outhouse."

The others laughed nervously behind them. Inching closer, Deb could make out the unmistakable form of a large dog lying on its back. Julie moved forward and shone a light on the animal. Crunch. Crunch. Legs wide apart, the dog playfully itched its back.

Realizing she had been holding her breath, Deb let out a sigh of relief.

"It's just a dog," she whispered towards the women behind her. "And it's cute."

"Oh for heaven's sake!" Julie answered. "We got worked up over that?"

The women turned around and walked back to the front door, swatting mosquitoes as they went. The dog followed and before they knew what was happening, the beast went to the rug in front of the fire, turned three circles and lay down as though it belonged in the room.

"Get that dog out of here!" Linda said. "I just swept the floor."

"Aww, look at him. He's happy!" Deb cooed.

"It's a girl," Julie said.

The dog was a full-grown golden lab. No gray hairs were encroaching on her muzzle. Sighing contentedly, the dog closed her eyes and went to sleep.

"I'm not making her leave," Deb said to the others. "You can if you want. For me, there are few sweeter sights in life than a content dog by a fireplace." The women shrugged and moved back to their seats, as the dog was soon temporarily forgotten.

"It's a good thing you didn't call the police," Deb teased, patting Carolyn on the arm.

"It's late," Carolyn said. "I'm going to bed. It's an early morning."

"Good night," the others called, as Carolyn retired.

"So, I remembered one thing we didn't do yet for the retreat. What are we going to do to make sure everyone knows where to go tomorrow?" Pat asked.

Julie smiled mysteriously and glanced at Noreen.

"Shall we tell them now?" she asked.

"Better now than tomorrow," Noreen replied.

The two women went into the bedroom and returned with a pile of poster boards already attached to stakes.

"Wow!" Pat looked at the pile. "Where did these come from?" she asked, reading the titles aloud:

RETREAT BREAKFAST AHEAD
Heavenly food at St. John's Church

PIE CHI HERE
Tai Chi with an Italian flair

WRITING WORKSHOP
Write the story you never wanted your husband to know

TAROT READING
Need an answer to a life question? Bev is your gal

SELF DEFENSE
Don't count on that male in your life to take care of you.
Learn to defend him!

DEB AND PAT'S CABIN THIS WAY

Everyone laughed.

"Great job!" Pat said.

"We got to thinking this afternoon that you might need some help with organizing," Julie said with obvious pride. "We thought we could have those of us who are not leading an event stationed around the signs to help direct the people. So we just tried this. We're a step ahead of you."

"More like half a mile, you mean," Pat replied, picking up a sign. "Oh, you women! I knew there was a reason we invited you along. You think of everything! But do we really need one that tells where we're staying?" she asked, pointing at the signs.

"'Fraid you're gonna get lynched?"

Pat smiled.

"Okay," Deb said. "With the ghostie and all, we forgot to talk about the missing woman. Did anyone hear anything?"

"I've got enough on my plate," Linda answered dismissively. "We're not the police."

"I'm not asking you to be; all I'm asking is for you to keep eyes and ears open... and mouths, too," Deb replied.

"That won't be hard for you, Pat," Julie joked, playfully punching Pat on the shoulder.

"What do you want me to do?" Linda asked, picking up a tablet and a pen from the table.

"Well, tomorrow there's going to be a breakfast at the church and the restaurants will be all full of hungry women. That should be a good time to do a little gumshoeing, you know, just quietly talking to people. Ask questions."

"Like about what they saw on the ferry?" Linda asked.

"Sure. But also about what they didn't see. Remember to be sure and write down quotes word for word. And don't forget to write down their names and phone numbers for each statement you get," Deb continued. "Otherwise, it will be useless afterwards."

"I can do that!" Linda exclaimed, as she meticulously wrote down the instructions.

"I'll make sure we make an announcement at Pie Chi," Julie said.

"And I'll be listening to the gossip during my art class," Noreen added.

"Tired?" Bev asked after the others had retired to the kitchen to clean up. She offered Deb a candy dish filled with mint chocolates.

"I'll be okay," Deb replied, sucking on a mint. "I'm still a little worried that we've forgotten something important. You know, that old 'responsibility' tape."

"I know what you mean, but just look at all you've done to get ready. You and Pat are two of the most industrious women I know. You must have put in a lot of hours, or days, getting ready. And you've got all of us."

"That's us, alright. Always working hard to chase our dreams."

"To live your dreams, you mean?"

Deb paused.

"Did you say *live?* What do you mean by *live your dreams?* I'm much better at being busy than living."

"Aren't we all?" admitted Bev.

"It seems to me there must be a few people in this world who know how to *really* live. Why is that anyway?"

"Now there's a question that's been asked forever."

"I'm getting closer to being about ready to push the 'done enough' button and let go. I'm just so tired of being the responsible grownup... then, to top it off, we manipulated our daughters into coming, and now they'll *really* know we're crazy!"

"Nothing you can do about that... Don't worry about a t'ing," Bev sang lightheartedly.

"'Cause... every little t'ing's gonna be alright," Deb joined in loudly.

"We heard that!" Julie's voice called from the kitchen. "No singing without us. We're coming in."

"What's going on in here?" Linda asked, drying her hands on a dish towel as she entered the main room.

"Oh, Deb's just trying to throw away her superwoman cape," Bev teased. "Come on in, and help us burn it in the fire."

"Deb! Were you sacrificing your joy again?" Pat accused, following the others from the kitchen.

"Not on your life, girlfriend!"

Thank goodness for levity, Deb thought.

"So here's what I know," Bev interjected into the quiet room.

"Drum roll, please," Julie joked.

"After I got M.S., it was like God was asking me to live... for *goodness* sake," Bev said softly.

"Live for goodness sake?" Deb repeated.

"Yes, as opposed to dying for the world's sake. That's what I thought

God wanted from me. Dying is easy, bit by bit, inch by inch: a P.T.A. meeting here; a little guilt there; a church council meeting; always doing the dishes; a load of self-sacrifice there. It's the living for goodness that's hard."

Noreen nodded in agreement.

"My priorities changed totally when I found out I was dying."

"So my question for you," Bev continued as she looked at them, "is are you willing to really *live* for the goodness of the world?"

"Let's just do a little practicing right now," Deb said. "Julie, stoke up that fire. I've got a cape to burn!"

"Wow, *this* is really going to be something! You two never do things half way, do you?" a voice called in the door.

Just what I need, Pat thought. *The mothers have arrived.* She put her hand on her forehead.

"Hello mother, glad you could make it," she said. *Please don't start,* she thought.

"We've come to help. What can we do? Are you settled in already? Do you have some coffee? I need mine in a cup with a saucer," Jessie said, her presence taking over as she walked slowly into the room.

Millie ambled in behind her, eyeing the table.

"I'll have what you're having," she said.

"Make that two," Jessie chorused.

Settling in around the table, the two older women looked around eagerly.

"So, really, how can we help?" Millie asked.

"Mom, you'll have to give us a minute," Deb stalled. "I don't know what you could do yet." She shook her head. "Lots, I guess."

Millie looked sympathetically at her daughter.

"Don't worry dear, I'll help you organize." She turned to Jessie. "She never was that great at it."

"Mom!"

"Listen," Pat said, jumping into the fray before her friend exploded. "We really just wanted you to just have fun, and you know, relax. Take a class or two. Learn something new."

"See. What did I tell you, Jessie?" Millie said with a heavy mother sigh. "I knew they would think we're too old to help."

"No, no, that's not it at all," Pat answered guiltily.

"Right," Jessie said, shaking her head. "So what do you need?"

"Well, we don't have anything for the kids yet..." Julie suggested. "What?" she asked, noticing the surprised faces of the others. "You know we need all the help we can get." She turned back to the mothers. "We don't have anything for the kids yet. Could you maybe read some books to them? The library will give you some to use, I'm sure. And it would be nice for the mothers, you know. They could get in a workshop without them."

The older women rolled their eyes at each other. Millie sighed again.

"Sure. Once again we're relegated to child care. Okay."

Millie stood up to leave. "Thanks for the drink. Just let us know the time and place and we'll let you know the title of our kid's workshop. We refuse to just be babysitters. Right, Jess?"

"Right. Besides we have to get going. We haven't checked out the Burned Down Café yet."

"Mothers!" Pat said after they left.

"Daughters!" Jessie said loudly, as the two white-haired women walked down the street. "Let's party!"

After everyone finally had done enough planning, Bev sat quietly in her room, arranging everything so that it was convenient for her. All the lights in the cabin were off and she could hear the sounds of snoring in the distance as she settled in for the night. She, however, was wide awake, so she sat on the edge of the bed and reached for a book from the pile of old journals.

I wonder if I can find a long lost relative like Carolyn, she mused. *I wonder if I want to.*

Thumbing through, she paused at a page.

"Why doesn't the toilet work in this place?" someone had written. She turned the page.

"Great place! Wish we could stay!"

That's boring. Hmm, here's one that looks interesting, she thought.

July 7, 1936

I've been reading these journals and just felt like I wanted to write my story, too.

Thank you for taking such good care of my boys and me. We came up a week ago when a friend invited us after their daughter was unable to join them. Being kind-hearted folks, they gave the cabin to us.

I was able to get off work from my waitress job and the boys were finished with school, so we decided to have a little fun.

We've been in shock from the death of my husband... shot dead in a bar by the owner after an argument. I have been sleepwalking ever since, just trying to take care of my four boys and put food on the table! Thank goodness I still have them! All they know is one day, their father was there and the next — he was gone forever.

There have been many days since

when I have wondered whether I could go on. I am so lonely. I just never thought it could happen to me.

I can relate to that, Bev thought.

My boys have been able to play on the beach, splash in the beautiful clear water and enjoy walking in the woods. It's another world away from our home in the city.

I was sitting in the cabin by myself after breakfast, feeling sad. The boys had gone for a hike looking for chipmunks.

There was a knock at the door. A visibly pregnant cleaning woman appeared, carrying clean towels. Such blessed luxury not to do laundry! I didn't know what I was supposed to do. A statue-like dog sat at her side.

"I came to clean your cabin.

Oh, blessed day, I thought. "Please come in, but let me help you. Don't strain yourself. I know how hard it is. I have birthed four young ones myself."

"Thank you kindly," she replied with an easy smile that lit up the room. "But it is a pleasure and my honor to serve you... Sit!" she told the dog.

Her words brought tears to my eyes. I have never been served by anyone in my life. It was all I could do to keep from squeezing her. But of course I couldn't do such a thing to a stranger.

Noticing my tears, she kindly asked what was wrong.

"I am just so tired," I replied.

"Please sit down," she invited.

I found myself telling her about my husband and boys.

"My mother always said I would experience losses in my life," I said, "but I never expected it to happen so soon. I never thought this would happen to me. I feel as though my life is nearly over."

I never thought this would happen to me, either, Bev thought.

Then, she said something really interesting.

"Your old life, you mean?"

As if she was my sister, we passed the morning without a thought to the boys.

"Maybe it's the fact that I am about to give birth," the woman said as we sipped tea. "But I have been thinking of midwives lately. I have decided that we women are all midwives in one way or another. It's our lot in life to birth life into the world and to help usher it out into the next. Your husband was fortunate to have a strong woman like you to be there at the end. It was a precious gift you gave him."

The woman reached over and touched my hand.

I didn't want to admit it then, but somehow I know that woman is right. When I was with her, I felt the presence of an angel. My spirit felt lighter and more peaceful as I sat there with her in the morning light. I dreaded her leaving.

I think her name might have been Mida.

I thought I would see her again but I didn't. Please bid her goodbye from a grateful mother and fellow midwife.

Yours,
Helen

Aren't we all midwives, Helen? Bev thought as she gently closed the book and laid it on the night stand next to the bed. Brushing her hair out of her eyes she reached for the mask to her breathing machine.

Why must there be so many losses in life? she wondered, remembering back over the years. She knew first-hand the indignities of inch by inch creeping loss of independence and bodily function.

We all have to respond to what the world gives us, she reminded herself. *Still, with the limited choices I have now, life is still worth it.* She pulled the blankets under her chin and closed her eyes.

"I must remember to write in a journal before I leave," she promised herself, just before floating off to dreamland.

Chapter Twelve
June 21

The sun was just coming up when Pat peeled open her eyelids.

Darn, someone's snoring woke me up just in the middle of a great dream. I wonder what time it is.

Stretching her arms over her head, she sat up in the log bed and looking around, saw no one else in the room.

Oops, I guess Mitch was right. I must snore. Damn, getting old is hell, she thought. *Of course I'm just sure it was a polite little sexy snore.* Ignoring the memory of her husband's voice a week earlier telling her she snored like a band saw, she stretched out in the comfy bed. *I could lie here all day. Maid, oh maid,* she daydreamed. *Could you bring me my fresh squeezed orange juice?* she pretended to call out. *Now you know I like it in a crystal glass.*

Suddenly, reality hit home like an icy washcloth in the face as she remembered where she was and why. Jumping out of the bed as adrenaline pumped through her body, she glanced at the clock.

"Glory halleluiah!" she said aloud.

Mitch had remarked a few days earlier that she seemed to be "damning" this and that a lot lately. And although she vehemently denied it to him, she knew in her heart it was true.

How could this be?

She didn't even like it when she heard other people swear. From childhood until college she had believed lightning would strike her dead if she used God's name in vain.

What had happened to her moral standards anyway?

Come on old girl, get a move on. Throwing on her new orange sweat suit, she hurriedly brushed her teeth and ran out the door, not caring much if it banged behind her.

Those other women will need to get up anyway. As for me, why did I promise to help with the big breakfast at the church?

Yawning, she looked around outside for the golf cart that Julie had rounded up the night before. Not seeing it in the driveway, she starting jogging down the street. Guilt is a great motivator, especially for Lutherans, and she'd had a lifetime to perfect it. She picked up her pace even more.

I hope I'm in time at least to help a little, she thought, her breath coming at an even cadence. Thanks to yoga and being on that damn treadmill I can do this. Shoot, I did it again... although I don't know if it really counts if it's only in my mind.

Running down the street, she waved to small groups of women, also making their way in the same direction. Pat stopped abruptly, almost running into the woman pastor in the dim light, who was carrying a large pile of plates.

"Oops, sorry," Pat panted out. "Can I help?"

"Sure, take these in, will you? And I'll get more from the car. Do you think we can have people eating outside?"

Pat looked around at the cool dim morning.

"Outside? Isn't it a bit cold?" she asked. *More like freezing,* she thought to herself.

"Maybe," the pastor replied over her shoulder, already on her way for another load of plates, "but frankly, this is going to be the best fundraiser this church has had in years. We don't want to turn away paying customers." She waved Pat toward the church door and bent over the back seat of the old Volvo to pick up another load.

Still panting a little from her run, Pat carried the box down the stairs into the church basement. She took a deep breath, taking in the smells of coffee brewing in the big aluminum pot, steamy buttery aromas coming from the oven, and bacon. Her mouth started to water.

There is something about the scents in church basements and kitchens that is like no others. Noticing the casseroles with covers all waiting in a row on a long table covered with a pink plastic table cloth, she laughed out loud. Even for breakfast the eggs couldn't just be fried up. They had to be served as hot dishes! It was a scene straight out of Garrison Keillor's imaginary *Lake Woebegone.*

The busy women in the kitchen ranged in age from about twelve to eighty five. They turned their eyes towards Pat curiously as they heard her laugh. Then, seeing it was just 'the crazy Lutheran pastor', they turned as one back to the serious work of feeding the multitudes. Hesitating, Pat shifted the heavy box to her other hip.

"Are you just going to stand there to admire our work, or are you here to help?" The gruff words were dispelled by the big grin on the islander's weathered face.

"Want them here?" Pat asked as she carefully placed the load on the end of the table.

"Yes, that's just fine."

"I'm here to help. Can I make more coffee?"

"No, no. We heard all about you. The word we got was that if we let you make the coffee you'll use so many grounds that our profit will be drunk up."

Laughter broke out all over the room.

"I guess my coffee tastes have preceded me. So be it," Pat said, pretending to be offended. "So what do you need?"

The women looked at each other as they continued their work.

Pastors aren't known for their kitchen skills, the islander thought, sizing Pat up. *But at least she's a woman and has that going for her.*

The woman would never say this to Pat directly, because, like the others, they were Midwesterners first and foremost and always polite.

"Tell you what," a woman about Pat's age said with a twinkle in her eye as she wiped her floured covered hands on her apron. "Why don't you be a money changer at the door for a while? You know, just take in the money. We know pastors are good at that!" There was even louder laughter this time. Pat joined in.

There is nothing like a church kitchen, that's for sure.

Walking over to the door she was surprised at the line forming outside. Women were dressed in everything from casual clothes to suits. All were smiling and chatting, trying to keep the cold wind out of their bones.

"Can I let them in?" she called out.

"Might as well. When we run out I guess we run out. First though, do you think we should pray? Lord knows we need the help."

"Pray to yourselves, then," the woman frying yet another pan of crispy bacon answered. "God will understand. He won't want us to serve a cold meal."

Opening the door, Pat gulped and then said a little prayer of her own, because the line of chattering women went all around the block.

Lord, I hope they remember that they all are watching their weight or we'll run out before half of them get through the door. Amen. Crossing herself, she motioned to the first group to come in.

"What are we charging?" Pat called.

"Mary, Mother of God, I don't know," came the reply from the elderly woman, not caring that the attendees could hear her every word. "Make it a free will offering, but hells bells, we better make enough to fix the organ. That thing wheezes like my old aunt Franny!"

Someone else has a little trouble with swearing, Pat thought, as she took the money from the first woman.

"Will ten dollars be okay?" *Yes,* Pat thought as she nodded her head, *I think the organ is going to get a new sound.*

After an hour or so of a steady stream, Pat went back to the kitchen.

"Can you get someone else to take money? It's slowed way down. I have to check on a few things."

"Oh, just put what you've collected in that drawer, and make a sign saying it's a free will offering. We've already made a great profit." The chief cook smiled. "Thanks for the help."

Pat did what any wise pastor does and followed the directions of the women in the church kitchen. She put the sign out and walked out the door.

Darn, I left my cell phone in my jacket, she thought, just as she bumped into someone.

"Sorry. Oh, Linda, it's you. Are you coming for breakfast?"

"No, you know me. I was up with the sun. I ate hours ago. But this is the place Deb asked me to try to get statements." She held out her notebook and pen. "I'm supposed to ask questions, and then report back."

"It's not really statements, Linda. We're not really detectives. Are you sure you don't mind? I want you to have some fun."

"Heck no. I don't have a class until..." she looked at her pad. "Ten thirty. I'm going to Noreen's watercolor class. This is fun. You didn't already ask people here yet, did you? This was supposed to be one of my spots."

"No," Pat assured her. "I was too busy collecting money. Happy hunting."

Linda fondly watched her go.

Good thing we're here to help.

Squaring her shoulders and using the loud occupational therapist's voice she saved for children, she called,

"Excuse me. If I could have your attention, please. As you probably know, the police think someone may be missing from the ferry."

A cacophony of voices responded with questions.

"That's all I know, too, really," Linda replied. "But I'm going to come to each of your tables to take down any information. Anything at all that you heard or saw."

"Like what?" came a voice from the rear.

"Like a woman you know that was coming and you haven't seen. Something that seemed odd or out of place to you."

"Are you with the police?"

"Oh no, just with the retreat. So I'll start over here, shall I? Thanks in advance for your help. Also, if you have information and don't have the time to wait or for some reason you don't want to tell me personally, leave it on the message board."

"Sure, we'll help," a woman replied...,"as long as it doesn't interfere with my ten o'clock massage."

Everyone laughed as Linda got to work, starting at the closest table.

Chapter Thirteen
June 21

"Hi, Pat! Coffee's comin' right up. Depth charge in it, right? Extra hot?"

Pat stood in the doorway at Lotta's, eager to put her feet up after serving breakfast to the multitudes at the church.

"Better make that with extra espresso. With all this craziness I might just need it," Pat replied, looking around at the crowded room and the line of women behind her.

"Suit yourself. Have a seat. I've been keeping that one for regulars." Lotta nodded her head toward a small table by the side of the counter.

"Thanks!" Pat replied, pulling out one of the sturdy wooden chairs and sitting down next to Bev.

Isn't it great that she thinks of me as a regular? Pat thought.

After she finished making the hot drink, Lotta handed the steaming cup to Pat.

"I'm taking a break. Come out and take over for me please," she yelled toward the kitchen. A young woman came out smiling at the line of women waiting to be served.

"What can I get you? Are you here for the women's coven event?" she asked one customer, taking her order.

"Hey!" Lotta gave the woman a stern look, before turning back to the table. She picked up a colorful quilt top about the perfect size for a newborn that had been setting on a bench.

"Beautiful," Pat said, "and it's not just in all pink or blue," she added approvingly. She savored her coffee as she watched Bev shuffle cards she held in her hands.

"How was the breakfast?" Bev asked.

"Crazy. How could this happen?" Pat whined

"If you build it, they will come. Or, in your case, if you invite them, they will come. Why are you so surprised?" Lotta asked. "Personally, I'm grateful. This time of year it's great to have the shop filled with folks. Do you know I had two women waiting for me to open this morning?" She stitched away at the colorful quilt.

"You won't find me complaining, either," Bev said. "I've got people signed up for readings almost the entire day. I even had to blank out time for lunch and a massage. By the way, thanks for bringing a masseuse out here. She's setting up after lunch and she's so busy, I could barely get in."

"What's wrong with me?" Pat replied. "It was my hair brained idea to have everyone come for solstice. Seriously, what a typically crazy thing to do. But, it's really a hoot, isn't it?" she added with a shrug of her shoulders.

"I know I'm coming for the bonfire, and I can't wait to get to your workshop on writing. Buck up. It's only a few days," Lotta encouraged. "What could go wrong?"

"So, do you want me to do a reading for you?" Bev asked after she finished shuffling the cards. She looked up at Pat with a smile. "It's on the house since you've brought me a lot of business." She held out the deck invitingly.

"Better watch out," Lotta teased her friend. "She has been reading the cards with such accuracy lately, people have been saying she's a witch."

"I'm not denying or confirming that rumor," Bev said with a grin. "Although there have been times when they've called me that with a slightly different spelling.

"So, want me to give it a try for you?" she asked, turning towards Pat. "I don't have a customer for half an hour."

Pat looked closely at Bev. *I've seen that true believer look projected many times on lots of religious fanatics,* she thought. *I'm just not sure I believe cards can tell my fortune. I have to be careful of Bev's newfound hobby, if that's what you call it.*

"What would your church women think about this?" Lotta asked.

"I'm not constrained by worrying about that," Pat said. My theology is pretty broad as long as it's for good purposes."

Bev's wheelchair was not noticeable until she pulled away from the table. Fiercely independent, her M.S. hadn't stopped her from traveling around both the inner and outer worlds. Her latest spiritual foray had been to learn the cards.

What the hell? Read my cards, you say? I'm the captain of my own ship, thank you very much, Pat thought. *But, if I wait much longer, Bev might be offended.*

With a consenting nod from Pat, Bev picked up her Rider's deck, an oversized pack of cards and placed them on the table. She handed the deck to Pat.

"What do I do?" Pat asked.

"Shuffle them," she said, "and cut the deck three times. We need your essence to go into the cards."

Right, Pat thought as she awkwardly shuffled the oversized deck.

Bev took the cards back after Pat finished.

"Tarot suits are different from your spades, hearts diamonds, and clubs. Do you know anything about them?"

"I've had readings before. Let's see. There were majors and minors and great pictures. I know there were Wands and Swords. And the Fool and Death."

"And Cups and Pentacles," Bev said encouragingly, as she held the deck in her hands."

"So, now what?"

"Now comes the mysterious part. We decide what to ask the cards."

Pat didn't even hesitate.

"What happened to the missing woman and who is she?"

Bev pulled a card from the deck.

"So, not one question, but two. Interesting, and, of course, how do you fit into this puzzle?"

After showing it to the other women, she laid it on the table.

"Pat, that's you," she pointed, "in the here and now."

Lotta returned to her quilting.

"Darn, I pricked myself. Hand me that napkin, will you, Pat?"

Pat reached out with a napkin, and saw that Lotta's finger was bleeding. As Lotta took the napkin a single drop fell onto the card.

"Sorry," Pat apologized, looking at Bev contritely. "At least it didn't get on the new quilt."

"You need to take this seriously," Bev admonished her. "Pat, these cards now have blood on them." She shivered. "Do you want me to continue?"

Pat looked at her with a chagrined expression.

"Of course. I mean, I'm sure it will be just fine. What is that card anyway?"

"Yes, funny isn't it? This is the card that kept coming up when I was learning and doing your reading. It's the Jester."

"You've been reading my cards?"

"Just practicing," Bev replied, her attention focused intently on the deck in her hands.

"Jester? Does that mean I'm a clown?"

"Hardly. The Jester represents the childlike ability to tune into the inner workings of the world."

"That sounds like me."

"Pick something else. She wants a good fortune," Lotta said, looking at the card and still dabbing her finger.

Pat leaned forward. "Is that one bad?"

"Don't encourage her. Bev will start over again. Or worse, she'll do full twelve cards, the most elaborate reading. You better have the time. Once she starts, she won't stop," Lotta warned.

"That's okay. I'm game. Do you really think you can read my future with the cards?" Pat asked skeptically.

"The question is, is she reading the cards or your face and body language?" Lotta asked. "You know what they say. Even a monkey can hit the right keys on a key board and spell a word now and then." She leaned over her quilting and held it toward the window. Her head was tucked down in concentration as her needle once again went in and out of the fabric.

"In case you're wondering, I'm making this for Bev's new granddaughter," Lotta said with a smile.

"She's a real artist, that's for sure. I read it in her cards. She always turns up the Empress, also," Bev said, concentrating on laying out the cards in a complicated pattern.

"I always wanted to be an Empress," Pat joked.

"The Empress can represent the germination of an idea before it is ready to be fully born," Bev explained. "Hmmm, Wow, the Five of Pentacles is reversed, and it's right next to the Chariot. Strange."

Putting down her cup, Pat pointed to a card.

"What's that one mean? It looks kind of like five swords. That looks positive, doesn't it?" she asked hopefully. The other two women exchanged a glance that made her feel uneasy.

"I just knew she would do this," Lotta said.

Bev ignored the comment and took a deep breath.

Sounding is if she were in a trance, she began the reading.

"The Tower stands for hidden evil... more than an enemy, more like a danger and confrontation, a battle. It's placed over your Jester so it's the main influence touching you or the missing person... you may be in a battle for this person, or she may be in a battle for something or someone else. In either case, it implies having to put oneself in danger to protect another."

"Gee, I'll bet you tell that to all your clients. You'd never make any tips if you did," Pat said playfully in an attempt to lighten the mood.

Without looking up, Bev pointed to another card directly above it. The Devil. She cleared her throat after pointing out the Devil card.

"This represents difficulties, problems to solve. And this one? Death." A heavy silence invaded the space. "This one means someone is missing, or left. Either forced or by their own free will. Gone. It can also represent new beginnings."

"Stop it, Bev. She doesn't need to hear all that stuff. She's got enough challenges these next few days."

"Yes... yes I do," Pat answered. "Go ahead."

Bev hesitated.

"Well, remember, I'm just new at this. Let's look this up."

She turned to her little book of helps and referring to the Death card, read:

This is one of the clearest cards when it comes to meaning. False structures, false institutions, false beliefs are going to come (or have already come) tumbling down, suddenly, violently and all at once. This sort of prediction can scare anyone, especially as the one you're reading for likely does not know that something is false. Not yet. To the contrary, they probably believe that there are no problems in their surroundings, that everything is fine at work... oh, and that they're fine. Just fine, really.

Alas, they're about to get a very rude awakening. Shaken up, torn down, and blown asunder. And all a reader can really do to soften the blow is assure the querent that it is for the best. Nothing built on a lie, on falsehoods, can remain standing for long. Better for it to come down so that it can be rebuilt on truth-or not rebuilt at all, if that's what seems best. This rude awakening is not going to be pleasant or painless or easy, but it will be for the best in the end.

"You could at least let her live until after this big solstice celebration," Lotta said sarcastically. "You know they burned women like her in the past, don't you?"

"Look! Here are two good cards," Bev continued. "This card at your feet says you are brave and true and this one at your right, the Star, means you will have help if you choose to use it."

"So that's good?"

"Well, not so good. Frankly, looking at the big picture, I've never seen so many negative cards, pardon me, challenging cards in one reading. Of course, I'm just a beginner, really," she added hastily, looking up and seeing Pat's face.

Pat glanced down at the cards laid out on the table. The coffee no longer tasted good in her mouth. Even to her untrained eyes the cards looked all dark and foreboding.

"Do you know where these challenges are coming from?" Pat asked.

"See this card here? It seems like it's sort of from a dark place out of time or space. It's confusing. Well, that's enough of that." Scooping up the cards, Bev quickly shuffled them as if to get rid of the reading entirely.

"You know you're in charge of your own life. And you don't need to worry. You're surrounded by women friends and family. What better protection could there be?"

"So, do you think you two could help with the serving tomorrow morning?" Pat asked. "The church ladies think we'll have to serve in shifts for the breakfast. You won't believe what a madhouse it was this morning at the church."

Neither woman balked at the request.

"I'd be glad to help you," Bev said. "With a Tarot reading like you just finished, you're going to need all the help you can get."

"I better get back to work," Lotta said.

"Look at the time," Pat said, standing up to leave.

"Say, Pat, before you go," Lotta said, catching them before they reached the door. "Did either of you leave this?" She held up a jacket. "It was left either last night or this morning, but with so many on the island..."

Pat looked at the designer jean jacket.

"Not me. Did you check the pockets?"

"Just quickly. I was too busy to do more."

Pat took the jacket.

"No, nothing in these pockets." She reached inside on the right side. "Nope, nothing here." She felt around one last time. "Wait a minute. Something is scrunched down in here. There, I've got it." Pulling out a torn slip from a waitress' order pad, she spread it on the table and quickly scanned it.

"No, no name, sorry." She looked closer at the note. "But this woman sounds like she's got a problem."

"Read it," Lotta and Bev said together.

"Okay." She read:

Sorry to leave you in a mess. That damn shit has just gone too far. Sure he's cute, but he threatened me because I was late after work last night. He even tried to push me down. Can you believe it? Happened to my mom; will never happen to me.

Will call soon. Love yah, girlfriend.

"There's no signature."

The women were quiet for a moment.

"Well, we can't find her from this. Sorry," Pat said.

"No worries. I'll just put it up on the message board," Lotta said.

"Message board? Since when has the island had a message board?"

"Us? Honey, we all know each other's business here. Small island, remember? No, this is the message board for your retreat. Linda put it up. "Better catch up, oh great leader," Lotta teased. "They're charging past you."

"Ain't that the truth?"

At that moment, Deb walked through the door into the crowded room.

"You should see what's happening out on the street!"

"Don't tell us. After my Tarot reading, I can't take any more," Pat joked.

"There's something I wanted to talk to you two about," Lotta said, hesitatingly.

"What is it?" Deb asked, noticing the tightness in Lotta's face.

"I'm not sure this is the right time. There's too much commotion now and I have to get working on lunch. Remind me later, okay?"

"Sure," Deb replied, making a mental note.

As Lotta walked to the kitchen, Deb and Pat joined Bev at the table.

"You really should see outside," Deb urged. "Someone put up a soapbox on the street with a sign that says, 'If you have something to say, say it here.' There's a line of women waiting to speak. Uh, oh," Deb whispered a few minutes later. "Here comes trouble."

Pat looked up and saw the all too familiar form of the handsome detective from Ashland County walk past the front window.

"Duck!" Deb whispered.

Before the women could duck, the door opened on a smiling Detective Gary LeSeur, who stood silently taking in the crowded noisy scene.

Dressed in jeans and tennis shoes, he wore a fishing vest and Brewers baseball cap. With laser-like focus, his flashing brown eyes met Deb's gaze and held it.

"Busted," Deb whispered.

With a nod of his head, he gestured toward the door.

"Excuse me," Deb said in a nonchalant voice. "I'll be right back."

Deb walked slowly toward the door as if summoned to the principal's office and into the presence of the law.

Deb and Pat had crossed paths with him on previous occasions when they had been involved in solving the mysteries behind two deaths.

Gary knelt just outside the door, petting a golden lab. The dog had been lying patiently in the sun just outside the door to the Café.

"Hi, Gary!" Deb said, trying her best to be cheerful. The dog stood immediately upon seeing Deb and wagged her tail so exuberantly against her that Deb almost lost her balance.

"Is that your dog?" LeSeur asked.

"No. She's just a stray that showed up at our cabin last night. We thought she was a bear in the dark..."

Damn. Why did I say that?

Gary stood up, as his perceptive gaze pierced through Deb's façade.

"So, what is this whole scene, anyway?" he asked, gesturing with his hands to the crowded dining room on the other side of the screen door.

"Just a little gathering that Pat and I tried to put together for summer solstice."

"You women don't do anything small, do you?"

"What are you doing here?" Deb asked reflexively.

"To be honest with you, this is the last place I would choose to be on a fine summer day as this... There I was, ready to get out on the big lake with my favorite fishing guide. My wife was gone to some women's retreat. Some girls-only event on the island. The weather was perfect. Things were quiet at the office and I took two days of vacation to try to catch up on my fishing. We no sooner got out and set anchor when I got a text message to call the office immediately. Something about a missing woman on the ferry.

"After talking to Mike and the crew, I thought I would just go to the eye of the hurricane and find out what you know. After all, you two started this whole mess by bringing all these women out here. And you always seem to be in the middle of things. So, tell me what you know."

"I really don't know much and what I know is secondhand," Deb replied reluctantly. "Really, I just know what you know... that the ferry people have some vague suspicions because of 'their counts' being wrong or something like that. Not a lot to go on."

"Well, let's get down to brass tacks then," Gary said. "Did anyone sign up for your 'retreat' and then not show up?"

"I couldn't answer that," Deb replied.

"Why not?"

"Because we didn't ask for signups. We didn't collect deposits or anything. This was supposed to be a small informal gathering. And then way more people came than we expected and the YouTube and all that we didn't expect," Deb rambled.

Like the fisherman he was, Gary threw another line.

"Did you have any speakers on your agenda that haven't shown their pretty faces out here yet?"

"Not that I know of," Deb replied. "Really, this was just supposed to be a simple, quiet getaway. But it's turned into something..."

LeSeur realized quickly that he wasn't going to catch any information from Deb and began to set his hook.

"Okay, Deb. I see you know nothing. But I also know how good you and Pat are at getting to the bottom of things. I need your help."

Hearing his words, Deb was momentarily speechless.

"You need our help? Mine and Pat's? Pat! Come out here!" Deb yelled into the crowded restaurant. "Gary needs our help!"

Pat walked briskly out into the sunlight with a confused expression on her face.

"Hi, Gary," Pat said. "What's happening?"

"He said he needs our help," Deb repeated.

Gary nodded his head.

"That's a strange turn, coming from you. What on earth do you want from us?" Pat asked.

"This place is so chaotic. I need you to ask around and talk to people who were on the ferry coming over yesterday when the incident happened."

"Incident? You call that an incident when someone is potentially dead?" Pat replied.

"Shh, Pat. He's only doing his job," Deb said. "Every investigation starts with an incident and an incident report, right Gary?"

Gary's face reddened as he chose to ignore the comment.

I will not respond to these crazies in kind, I am better than that, he thought.

"There's no way we have the resources to talk to every one of these women," he said. "I need you to winnow out the ones who may have any information at all. Remember, its first-hand information I want, not gossip."

"We can try," Pat said. "Just leave it to us."

Shaking his head, Gary handed his business card to Deb.

"Here's my cell number. Make me a list of names and contact numbers and get back to me as soon as possible."

"Aye, aye, captain!" Pat replied in mock salute.

As Gary strolled away towards his waiting fishing boat, Deb turned to Pat.

"Can you believe he asked us for help this time?"

"Can you believe we would agree to help?" Pat answered.

"There's just one thing I wanted to tell you."

"What?"

"Remember that woman we met on the ferry when we were coming over before the retreat started?

Pat paused. "You mean Windcatcher?"

"No, the one who helped me up when I fell."

"What about her?"

"She's been sort of haunting me."

"Oh, Deb, you have a too rich imagination."

"Maybe. Or maybe not."

"Well, if it worries you, you can always tell Gary about her."

"I probably will."

Chapter Fourteen
June 21

Pat walked back to the cabin to change her shirt, as the dog followed her.

"I'm staying behind to set up the writing workshop," Deb called. "Remember, we have to lead it today."

"Okay, I'll be right down," Pat said louder than necessary into the phone a few minutes later as she entered the door.

Remember what Swami Ji, the Yoga master, said she told herself as she hung up the phone. *Breathe. Just breathe. In with the calm clear air, out with the... what the hell is happening down at the self defense class? It sounds like all hell has broken loose. It's a damn good thing I didn't put out a glass jar to put a dollar in every time I've sworn, or I'd be broke before the day is over.*

"Oops I did it again. I'm outta here!" she yelled to no one in particular. "The gods of chaos are laughing today, that's for sure."

Slipping into her new tennis shoes, she ran out the door leaving a confused dog alone in the cabin. The dog popped her head up from the couch where she was catching a snooze.

She huffed out the fine hairs around her muzzle as if in a laugh. "Humans! Who can figure them out?" she seemed to be saying in dog language as she laid her head back down and settled in for a nice long nap.

Pat climbed onto the golf cart that Julie had managed to place in the driveway for her, and went bumping down the street. Along the way, she met Bev sitting outdoors under a colorful Thai umbrella at the station she was assigned on Bell Street. Her electric scooter was festooned with ribbons flying in the breeze. Pat waved at Bev who was doing a reading for another woman seated in front of her.

Waving back gaily, Bev turned her attention to the business at hand. The other woman's worried face made Pat hope Bev was remembering the first rule of good card reading. *Never scare the pants off your client.* She noticed that Bev, in spite of all the work, looked ten years younger.

"Wow that line is getting long!" Pat called out, noticing women waiting patiently for a turn. Immediately, she regretted her words. But, instead of looking worried or tense, Bev looked energized.

"Yeah, isn't it great? Bev called back. She turned back to the woman in front of her.

"This card may look bad, but it really is a good card for change," she said.

Pat flew by the crowd and continued on her way.

I can't believe a person sometimes has to face their own mortality before they can begin really living.

She slowed for a gaggle of older women crossing the road to go into the Mission Hill Coffee Shop when she heard a familiar voice ahead and off to the right.

"That's right ladies, take your can or your water bottle, whatever you have, and just dip it right into the lake there. What could be better than to have a watercolor painting with a bit of the big lake right in it?" Noreen called out.

Dutifully, about seventy-five women walked into the icy cold water, giggling and gasping. They dipped their hands in the lake to get water, which to Pat, resembled a massive baptism scene. Pat drove on.

That Noreen. How like her to make a simple act of getting ready to paint into an almost spiritual event. Every time those women from all over the world look at the painting they created, they'll remember the big lake.

Nearing a beach along the way, she slowed down.

What a pretty sight, Pat thought, as a tiny girl, her innocent face lit with joy, stepped onto the sand, putting a cautious toe into the chilly water. Instead of wearing a bathing suit, she had on a bright yellow dress that danced in the breeze. Her toe nails were painted different colors.

"Why all the colors? Couldn't you pick?" Pat called out, drawn by the child's innocence and hoping to make contact.

Turning slowly, the child looked seriously first at her toes and then at Pat. To her surprise and delight, Pat realized it was Gracie, Deb's granddaughter.

"No, it's because I like all the colors so I used them all." She laughed as she ran up to Pat. "Don't you just love them?" she asked. She was already both sure of the answer and sure of herself.

"Yes, I do. Did you come with someone?"

"Of course, silly." She laughed again. "I'm just a child!" "There's Mommy over there," she pointed. "We came to your party to pray." She shifted from one foot to the other as if eager to dance.

"To pray? What for? Do you want a puppy, or a surprise?"

"Oh, no, for goodness sake."

"Excuse me?"

"I heard about it from some girls who live here and Mommy says we can do it, too."

"The children told you they pray?" Pat asked with interest.

"Yes, and they invited me back next year." She came closer and whispered, as if to share a secret. "We pray her back."

"Back?" Pat frowned. "Did someone go somewhere?" Startled, she thought of the missing woman.

"Must have, don't know. But she has a nice name. Want to hear it?"

"Sure. If it's okay for you to tell me."

"It's Hope. Isn't that pretty?" She tapped her little foot as if Pat were a bit slow.

"So. How do you pray? Is it like on your knees or do you read it out of a book?"

This time her laughter was like little bells on the wind. "You know."

"I'm afraid I've forgotten a long time ago. Remind me," Pat encouraged.

"You sing it, or dance it, or just laugh it out loud." She stared sympathetically into Pat's eyes. "Just try. Even old people can remember how."

Thanks a lot, Pat thought. "Is there anything else I should know?"

"Well, I think... nobody told me, but I think it works better in a bunch. Together."

"Together?" *Where two or more are gathered,* she thought.

"You can do it alone, but hope works better together because when you're bad, you want to be alone and hide, right? But when you're good..."

"You want to share it?"

"Right." She ran off to play with the lake.

Pat felt much better. *I wonder who this Hope is that she was talking about. Or is it hope they pray for?* Putting her thoughts aside she continued on her way.

Stepping on the pedal, Pat raced past St. John's church and then slowed for the large crowd ahead of her.

It must be the crazy full moon or something, she thought, surveying the scene. Driving into the agitated crowd, Pat stopped and jumped off the cart, as one woman helped another one up off the ground.

"You said I should show you how it was done," the standing woman said to one on the ground.

"Right, like I meant throw me half way across the island?" the now standing woman huffed as she dusted herself off.

"Ladies, ladies. What the heck is the matter? And where is your instructor?" *She had better not have panicked and run away is all I can say or she'll owe me a tall one when this is over. Sure she can handle thieves and a wife abuser, but a crowd of women learning self-defense? How much could you ask of a policewoman?*

"Oh," said one tiny grey-haired woman helpfully. "She had to take a young girl to the Doc."

"To the Doc? What happened?" Pat turned to the two women in the center of the crowd. "Did one of you hurt her?" she asked with her hand placed accusingly on her hips. *Goddess,* she thought exasperatingly, *what is this world coming to?*

"Us? No! How could you even think that?" they said together, united in the face of Pat's anger. "No, this girl came by on her bike and fell and hurt her knee. Our teacher asked us to keep things going till you got here."

Oh, great, Pat thought. "Did she give you any other instructions?"

"Just like not to kill each other, or break anything," someone said with a giggle. "She said the Doc was busy enough with the pregnant woman."

"Pregnant woman?!" Pat asked incredulously. Then she let out a heavy sigh. "Never mind. I don't actually want to know. Anyone know about self-defense here?"

There was silence except for the sound of the waves. Hesitantly, a woman of about eighty-five raised her hand part way up.

"You are in charge," Pat said as she pointed at the woman. "Show them some moves and whatever you do..."

"Don't kill each other or break anything," several women called out. Everyone laughed.

Getting back on her cart, Pat tooted her little electric horn cheerily at the women.

"Now count off in twos and stand like this facing each other," she overheard a surprisingly vigorous voice say.

The last thing Pat saw in her rearview mirror as she drove away was the image of the tiny woman soundly throwing her hapless partner onto the ground.

Wow, the marina is full today, Pat thought, as she drove down the dirt road toward Coole Park. *Some of the women must have sailed over. I might as well check in on the croquet tournament as long as I'm down here. It'll be great to see at least one thing happening as it's supposed to.*

"Hey, Pat," a voice called from the woods to her right. She slowed and stopped as Mike's wife approached her. "Have you made any headway on that missing woman?"

Pat shook her head.

"Truth is, we've been pretty busy with all the women who are not missing," she said, waving her hand in reference to the whole island.

"Busy? It's more like this would be a special hell reserved for micromanagers." Noticing Pat's reaction, the woman smiled reassuringly.

"Don't worry. Everyone seems to be having fun. It's a real happening, like the sixties, only no sex and drugs." She patted Pat on the shoulder. "But seriously, it would be a big help if the authorities knew for sure the woman was or wasn't part of the retreat crowd. Mike's been going crazy with guilt that someone might have been lost on his watch."

"I know, I know. Gary has asked us to try to help him find out more about it. Truth is, we can't tell who half these crazy women are. Our registration sort of went by the wayside after the fifth or sixth boatload of women arrived. I wish I could be more help. Tell Mike when you hear from him that we're doing the best we can."

After setting up materials for the writing workshop, Deb decided to go for a walk.

I don't feel like going back to see how the classes are going just yet. I don't feel like doing anything, really.

She meandered around, until she found herself at the golf club, up on the hill on the eastern side of La Pointe. She sat down on a bench, looking out over the top of the town to the beautiful lake.

I don't think I'll ever go on another retreat, no matter who leads it. For that matter, I don't think I'll ever listen to one of Pat's dumb ideas again.

The lake was beautiful to look at and so was the town. In every direction Deb looked there was something going on for the retreat. She could even see Pat in the distance driving off towards Coole Park Resort on the silly golf cart she had commandeered.

I only wanted to have a little fun, she thought. *I just wanted to feel younger and more carefree for a few days. And darn, not only has the retreat gone cockeyed, but there's that missing woman.*

She had a feeling someone needed her right then, but she sat stubbornly for a moment anyway. Looking at the waves sparkling like diamonds, and boats bobbing, she felt herself relax.

There must be a God or a Goddess, or something anyway, to make such a beautiful place and to keep it from harm. Deb is a believer who has a deep-seeded belief in goodness.

"Mind if I sit?"

Looking over at a native woman standing by her side, she moved over.

"No, of course not. I'm just trying to take a breather, from it all."

"The retreat, you mean? I know. You're one of the organizers, aren't you? I was just at the painting class. It was great. That Noreen really knows how to get people going. And she is so respectful of the lake. I'm sure the lady was smiling at her."

"The lady?"

"Yes, you know. We islanders have always believed in the lady who protects it. She is said to renew everything on each summer solstice. I don't know if it's true, but it's a nice story."

"Is it supposed to be Madeline, the woman who the island is named after?"

"Well, that was her Christian name, given to her by a black robe so that she could marry a French man. Some say it's her, but the legend seems to go back longer than that."

"Who do you think it is?"

"Me? I don't think about it much. We celebrate the renewal of spring at solstice, and it brings hope. That's enough for me. But when I was a child, I once thought I met her."

"Really?"

The woman laughed with embarrassment. She paused.

"Yes, I was frightened one night. I had stayed a little too long on the beach, not listening to my mother, don't you know? It was dark. The darkness almost took a shape and I was too scared to go home on the lonely dirt road. I started to cry. Then a woman came. A woman about my mother's age. She took my hand and smiled. And then it didn't seem so dark anymore. She just took me right to my door."

"Was it the spirit, do you think?"

"Could have been. Even if it wasn't, she got me home safe, but didn't keep me from a smack on my behind for being late." She chuckled at the memory. "Who knows how legends start up? Maybe you and your friend will become one after this weekend."

"Well I certainly hope not! Have you heard about the woman who is gone from the ferry?" Deb asked.

The woman nodded.

"What do you think happened?" Deb prodded.

"I think sometimes things happen and we never know why. Maybe she just lost hope, or maybe she was taken up to the sky. After all, you Christians believe in the rapture, don't you?"

"I believe in something more, but whether I think she was taken up to heaven, well, that doesn't seem real to me."

"Maybe not, but if you keep your eyes open, sometimes you see a lot more."

Deb looked out over the beauty of the vast hills before her.

"In my experience, things always seem impossible until someone makes them happen," the woman continued. "Like your retreat. Look at all these women, together, enjoying the island and each other. They will all take this experience away from here and some will share it. Out, out, out, it will go like waves on the big lake. Goodness spreading. Now that is something that some might think is impossible."

Deb could only nod her head in agreement, feeling better about her dream.

I guess I won't kill Pat, after all, she thought.

The women sat together on the bench in companionable silence.

Pressing her foot on the pedal once more, Pat looked ahead down the dusty road toward the croquet field.

"I have to go see how the croquet tournament is going." Waving goodbye to Mike's wife, she turned into the double drive of the old lodge.

Putting along, Pat noticed several women sitting sedately on benches in the gazebo and others on blankets on the lawn next to the croquet field.

Now this is what I thought this retreat would be like.

Relaxing a little, she slowed and smiled at the women as she passed. One or two were so relaxed they were actually sleeping. Or were they? Pat slowed to a crawl.

Wait a minute. That woman fell asleep with a wine glass still in her hand. Could she possibly be ill?"

Setting the brake, Pat climbed off the cart and walked over to the two women. Both of them were out like lights. She gently reached down and shook a shoulder of the first woman. The woman slumped over.

Good Lord, have they been poisoned? she thought as she knelt down to lay the woman out flat. One whiff at close range was all she needed to let Pat know what was wrong. *What?* Not sure if she was relieved or angry, Pat quickly realized that no matter how much she shook the women, she would not be able to rouse them. They would just have to sleep it off.

Looking around the bucolic scene, Pat realized with growing dread that everyone she could see, walking, sitting, and dancing in the field before her weren't just happy and relaxed. They were HAPPY.

"Great retreat," called out a woman. Pat recognized her as a pillar of the Lutheran church in Ashland. The woman weaved as she walked. "Who would have thought a women's spiritual retreat could be so much fun?" Raising the glass she held in her hand, the woman yelled out one final toast. "Here's to the moon!" she said as she continued on down the road.

"Would you look at that?" Pat murmured aloud to herself. She leaned against the cart as if for support and pulled her iPhone from a jacket pocket, pressing the quick dial to Deb.

"Pick up Deb, pick up." After a minute, Pat heard Deb's granddaughter's little voice.

"Hi, this is Gracie." A giggle. "Grammy says she's busy, so leave a message."

Now, what are we going to do? Pat thought.

Saying goodbye to her new acquaintance, Deb headed to her massage appointment. She had reserved the time before coming out to the island and had meant to cancel it when all the commotion started. Refreshed from her time away, she decided to keep it.

She was soon lying on a warm blanket out in the open air. She had allowed only a short time for herself. Ten minutes into the massage, she felt a vibration against her leg as she lay prone on the table in the front screen porch at Lotta's Café. Warm rocks had been placed strategically over pressure points on her back only moments earlier by the busy therapist. She roused momentarily from her drowsiness.

"Damn! I'm so sorry I forgot to turn that off," Deb said into the room.

"Don't worry about it," a woman replied from the table next to her. "At least you have someone who wants to get a hold of you. Unlike me. Some days I wonder what the point is of being married when my husband couldn't care less. Matter of fact, he has no idea where I am right now."

"Where are we, anyway?" Deb asked dreamily from her fog.

The masseuse placed more rocks on Deb's neck and shoulders.

"So, did you hear about the missing person yesterday?" the woman asked. She turned over, facing Deb, and propped her head on her hands.

"I heard something about it," Deb replied, annoyed by the unwelcome intrusion into her dream state. "What do you know?" she asked, slowly being drawn back into the room.

"Me? Well, I know who it is!" the woman announced confidently.

"What?" Deb reacted, sitting up suddenly. As she did so, the rocks rolled noisily to the floor with a thud. "What do you mean, you know who it is? Tell me more," Deb insisted.

"Well," the woman replied, stroking her chin with well manicured nails. "She's my neighbor."

"Your neighbor?" Deb responded incredulously. Peering into the dim light, Deb could see that the woman wore a cultured pearl necklace and earrings. "Where do you live?"

"Here on the island. I have this neighbor woman who comes and goes several times a day and now, all of a sudden, she's gone. I haven't seen her for nearly two days."

"That's it?" Deb replied with a deep sigh as she lay back down on the table. "Uh, sorry about that," she gestured with her finger to the harried masseuse who was on her hands and knees on the floor searching for a missing hot rock. The woman gave Deb an exasperated look.

"I guess I better go get more rocks," she muttered.

"Why would anyone leave the island at this beautiful time of year?" Deb asked.

"Probably humiliated to face me after what I witnessed earlier this week."

"What was that?" Deb asked, suddenly feeling an unwelcome familiarity with this complete stranger.

"Well, I had just returned on the ferry from the mainland. I had to go to Ashland for my botox; a girl has to keep herself looking good, you know. When I got back, I heard my husband talking in the bedroom. I thought he was talking to the maid so I didn't think anything of it.

'Honey, I'm back,' I called. I heard a scrambling sound and the closing of the bathroom door and I walked in to find him pulling up his jeans. I walked over to the bathroom door and opened it.

'Maria, is that you?' I called. It wasn't Maria. It was my neighbor wrapped in nothing but a towel, the same towel I had used that morning. Can you believe the nerve of that?"

Deb could see that the woman was fiddling with her pearls as she spoke.

Why do people tell me these things? Deb thought.

"That must have been really hard on you," she commiserated.

"You're not kidding! I paid a minor fortune for that towel. It was made of hemp."

"If I found something like that at my house, I'd be tempted to hurt someone."

"Oh, I'm used to this drama," the woman replied forlornly. "I've put up with it my entire marriage, nearly ten years now."

"How can you be so blasé about something like that?" Deb wondered aloud.

"Oh, baby, believe me. The truth is, I'd have knocked her off the boat myself if I'd have been there yesterday," the woman replied savagely. "It's no wonder that woman left when she did. I am certain that the authorities are wasting their time looking into this. That woman left. She's not dead," she rambled into the air, as if trying to convince the dust mites. "She's too mean to be dead. At least, I didn't kill her."

Realizing that she had once again been drawn too far into someone else's drama, Deb turned her attention back to the hot rocks and put her head back on the table. Making a mental note to herself to discuss the woman with Gary, Deb's body began to melt into the massage table like molten gold.

"You won't believe this one, kiddo. Call me," Pat said, leaving a voice message for Deb. She returned her cell to her pocket, staring hard at the scene around her, and hoping to somehow change it. Before her, the beautiful Victorian croquet field lay in shambles.

Stumbling over a cast iron wicket, she noticed Julie sitting alone on a pretty white bench that was usually reserved for spectators. She was either in shock or in awe of the whole scene. Pat couldn't tell which.

"What happened?" she asked as she approached. She lifted a hand-crafted mallet from the ground and gently leaned it against the bench. Julie turned toward her as if in a daze.

"I had to stop the tournament. I couldn't trust them with the mallets and the wooden balls. One woman actually used the mallet like a baseball bat and hit a ball right over the fence." She looked skyward as if she was seeing it all again. "Pretty good hit, I must say."

They sat together quietly for a minute.

"Where did all the wine come from?" Pat asked, breaking the silence at last.

And how in the hell will we ever pay for the damages? These people will never let us have a retreat here again!

Julie shrugged as if just realizing that Pat was there. "Oh, you know, Coole Park supplied some. They always do that as a courtesy. But the women brought bottles. Lots of them." Putting her head in her hands she let out a moan.

"It all started out so well, really. Then one lady suggested that when you missed the hoop you had to have a drink of wine. Soon, each time someone missed, everyone took a sip." She looked through her fingers at Pat who nodded encouragingly for her to continue. "And they weren't very good players you see. Balls were going every which way. No one took turns, and all it took was someone yelling 'missed ball' and down went the wine."

"Honestly," she added, "I don't even think they waited for someone to really miss the ball. They just called it out!"

Pat put her arm around Julie and picked up a half empty bottle from beside her.

"Missed ball!" she said and took a swig and handed it over. Julie took a big gulp and they then both started to laugh, passing the bottle back and forth. After a few minutes, the bottle was empty. They stood up.

"Come on. It won't take us very long to at least pick this court up a little before the owners see it."

A serious looking young woman walked briskly up to them, carrying her own mallet in a case.

"Is this where the tournament is?" the woman asked, oblivious to the chaos.

"Honey," Pat said, looking her straight in the eyes. "The tournament was such a success everybody won!"

"What was the prize?"

"An afternoon nap," Julie answered as she looked straight at Pat.

They didn't stop laughing for a very long time. Not appreciating the humor in the situation, the young woman moved on.

Pat felt a vibration of her cell phone on her leg just then.

She chose not to answer it.

Chapter Fifteen
June 21

After her massage daze wore off, Deb walked back toward the cabin. Off to her right, on the lawn outside the public library, she spied a gathering of young girls seated on colorful blankets.

Two white-haired women were perched in lawn chairs in front of the girls. Piles of books were scattered on the ground.

Oh, there's Mom and Jessie doing their workshop, Deb thought, pleased with the turnout.

As she neared the gathering, she read a sign posted over the door behind the elders: "Exploring the Female Warrior: Girls are Strong Too!"

Wow, we really are doing something right here, Deb thought. *I wish we could have had a session like this for our girls when they were younger.*

Approaching the group quietly, Deb stood behind a large oak tree, trying to overhear.

"Even in the Bible, there were women warriors," Millie explained. Standing for emphasis, she raised a long cardboard sword in the air. "There was even one woman in the Bible who saved her village by putting her sword into the head of a..."

"Mother!" Deb blurted out.

The girls all turned around to stare at a red-faced Deb. Millie's glare met Deb's.

"These girls need to know that they have power to use for good," Millie said quietly.

"We'll talk about this later," Deb said, choosing not to make a scene.

"Run along, dear," Jessie said. "We have this in hand." She blew kisses at Deb as she walked away, shaking her head.

I wonder how many complaints we'll get from unhappy mothers about this workshop, she thought. She straightened her shoulders. *I don't really care. If we can't trust our mothers, who can we trust?*

"Gramma, let me have the sword. I can do it!" Deb could hear Gracie calling out as she walked away.

Maybe I better check on things down at the camp, Deb thought, hastily retreating from the scene.

Nearing the beach across from the church, a small group of tents were pitched close together, providing temporary shelter to latecomers without lodging.

A young woman lounged on a cot outside the first tent.

"How is everyone doing here?" Deb asked. "Are you getting enough to eat?"

"Are you kidding? I'm going to have to diet from all the food just from today," the woman said, holding her stomach. "The Beach Club was putting out free fish livers for lunch. You should have seen all the women there. It was like seagulls going after chum behind the fishing boats."

Things seem to be okay here, she thought.

Smiling at the image in her mind of women vying for fish livers, Deb waved and walked towards the Ferry Dock. A truck pulled up beside her.

"Need a ride?" a woman asked from behind the wheel. Deb recognized her as an employee of the Pub, one of the local restaurants.

"Sure," Deb said. "I'm headed for the ferry.

"Hop in. I'm going there myself to pick up supplies for dinner."

The woman drove onto the dock just as the four p.m. ferry arrived. A large throng of women walked off ahead of the vehicles onboard.

"Where is this damn retreat, anyway?" a voice asked.

"Why aren't there any signs here?" another grumbled.

"Where's the taxi?" called a third.

Oh, Lord, Deb thought. *They're still coming. When will they stop? What do they think this is, anyway?*

She pulled out her notebook and made a note to herself to station more volunteers at the dock for the duration of the retreat.

"Did you hear about the missing woman?" the truck driver asked.

"I did," Deb answered, as she helped the woman lift large boxes of produce into the back of the truck.

"Did they figure it out yet?"

"As a matter of fact, they're still trying to determine if it was a mistake or not."

"I heard that someone jumped."

"That's always a good story. But I'm hoping not," Deb replied soberly. She looked at the clock on her phone.

"I have to get to my writing workshop. Thanks for the ride."

I hope Pat is there already, she thought as she hurried towards town.

Deb walked quickly over to the picnic tables set up on the patio outside the Bell Street Tavern, relieved to see that Pat was already handing out papers and pens to several women.

She was glad to see so many women attending and hurried to catch up.

"I am Pat, and this is my late friend, Deb. For the next few hours, we are going to help you harness your creativity and discover that you really can write, and we're not going to waste any time getting started. We're going to jump right in, because that is the best way to overcome any fears we may have about our ability. Deb, here, is going to read you the beginning of a short story and you will have just six minutes to finish the story... remember that you can be or do anything in this story. Let your imaginations go wild. Take it away, Deb."

Deb shot Pat a grateful look and picked up the outline from the table and read the story of a woman and a box aloud in a clear, loud voice.

"Ready, ladies, pick up your pens and finish the story," Deb concluded. She watched the scene as each woman hesitated briefly and then began to scribble frantically on the papers before them.

This is what a writing workshop is supposed to do, Deb thought with satisfaction, noticing the women growing in confidence before her eyes as they wrote enthusiastically the entire time allotted.

Invigorated by the success of their workshop as evidenced by the eager sharing of their writings by the participants, Pat and Deb sat in the cabin with their friends afterwards, a pitcher of Vodka Slushes close at hand.

"Well, we made it through our first day!"

Deb raised her glass.

"I had one hundred-fifty people at my two art sessions," Noreen said. "It was crazy, but nobody complained." Noreen took a long sip. "Man, this tastes good." And to think a year ago, I couldn't taste anything.

"You won't believe who talked to me while I was having a massage," Deb said.

"You had a massage in the same room with someone else? Eeww!" Carolyn said.

"What?" Pat teased. "Did LeSeur and his buddies stage a raid at Lotta's?"

"Nothing that good. I met this really angry woman having a massage next to me."

"Oh, that was relaxing," Pat said.

"Why was she angry?" Noreen asked.

"Oh, you know," Deb said. "Her husband was screwing around."

"Ow," Linda said.

"That's not the worst of it," Deb said. "He was doing it with the other woman in her bedroom, and she caught the woman in her own bath towel."

"Eeww," they all said together.

"That's quite a drama," Pat said. "What did you say to her?"

"Oh, just sympathy and all that. After all, I was in massage bliss from the hot rocks. And I was more struck by the woman's attitude than the gory details."

"What do you mean?" Pat asked.

"This is why I'm telling you the story. The woman acted absolutely convinced that the missing woman from the ferry is her husband's mistress."

"Why do you think she would think that?"

"She said that the woman never leaves the island and all of a sudden she seems to have disappeared."

"That's easily explainable," Linda said. "Wouldn't you hide out and not show your face if your neighbor found out you were sleeping with her husband? I don't know how I could show my face. I'd probably leave too."

"Could be," Deb replied. "I just wonder if she could have been behind the woman's disappearance."

"Why would you think that?" Pat asked.

"She just seemed so angry. Her anger just felt so hot and violent. You should have seen her!"

"Oh, Deb, you were probably having a hot flash," Pat said. "It's probably nothing but the usual run of the mill tale of a broken heart."

"Just wallowing in the muds of vengeance," Linda agreed. "Wouldn't both the husband and the wife have reason to make their neighbor disappear? After all, if the wife divorces the guy, she would lose her comfortable lifestyle, right?"

"That's motive," Julie said.

"Here," Linda said, pulling out a pen and sheet of paper. "We're going to make a chart of suspects."

"Wait a minute," Deb interrupted. "Before we do that, I want to tell you something else. Maybe there's more to this than just facts and suspects."

"What do you mean?" Bev asked.

"After my massage, I walked over to the golf course to take a break," Deb explained. "I met a woman there who sat with me for awhile. We actually had a deep discussion."

"That's nothing new for you," Bev said.

"So, what does she have to do with this?" Linda asked.

"If you wait a minute, I'll tell you."

"Was it someone from the retreat?" Noreen asked.

"She said she attended your watercolor class. She told me she really liked it."

"What did she look like?"

"Long dark hair, high cheekbones..."

"Was she Native?" Noreen asked.

"She looked to be. She was definitely an islander... she told me about this oral tradition passed down by the elders."

"Tell us," Julie urged.

"She said that there's some 'spirit woman' that some islanders believe in who protects the island... sort of like a guardian angel. She's supposed to bring renewal at summer solstice."

"Do, do, do, do, do, do, do, do...," Carolyn hummed. "That sounds pretty far out."

"That's what I thought at first," Deb said. "But the woman shared this personal story with me about an encounter she had on the island as a child. It seemed authentic enough to me."

"What would this spirit woman be doing on a ferry boat, then?" Carolyn asked. "Assuming that she's the missing person."

"It's solstice. Maybe she goes off the island then and comes back," Deb said. "My instincts tell me there may be something to it."

"I don't believe it," Carolyn said firmly.

"Deb's instincts have always been pretty sharp," Bev said.

The women pondered this for a few minutes.

"My instincts tell me that perhaps we should look beyond the here and now to try to explain the missing woman," Deb continued.

"Sounds too Zen-like for me," Carolyn said. "Maybe, we'll never know the answer."

"That's just what the woman said," Deb replied softly.

"So, we'll put the woman from the massage and the spirit woman on the list of suspects," Linda said. "Does anyone else have any suggestions?"

"I probably should tell Detective LeSeur about the woman at the massage next time I talk to him," Deb said.

"Okay, so tomorrow..."

Pat's phone rang.

"Sorry, scuse me. Hello," she said, talking into her phone. "Oh, hello, kiddo, are you on your way?" There was a pause as she listened.

"Daughter," Deb mouthed to the others.

"Yes, oh I understand. Work is busy. And the dog has to be boarded.

Uhuh, uhuh. Sure no, oh, of course. But there's this thing...," Pat hesitated. Glancing up, she saw Julie elbow Noreen.

"You see, you said you were going to be here so I sort of got you a gig."

"Gig! Mother!" Everyone at the table overheard. "Just a wee one, daughter. It's at the Burned Down Café, and I only signed you up for a fifteen-minute set. Well, actually two fifteen-minute sets, but they're separated by an hour and a half so you can just do the same one over."

She listened for what seemed like a full minute. Deb shook her head sympathetically and poured her friend another slush.

"Yes dear, well thanks. I know you'll just knock 'em dead. Your second cousin is playing the keyboard for the singers. Here, let me give you her cell." Finding the number, Pat repeated it into the phone. "I'll meet you at the dock, tomorrow morning at ten. Love you." She paused and lifted her glass, "Whew... I knew that would get her here."

"You are so devious." Noreen said. "By the way, why were those swords laying on the ground in the babysitting area?"

"You really don't want to know," Deb answered.

Deb's phone ring interrupted them.

"Hello, this is Deb. Oh, hi, daughter. Do you know which ferry you're coming in on? I see... school is busy, you've got a paper to write, I see... the thing is... I did sign you up to give that little talk on Vegan Made Easy that we talked about." Pausing to listen, she held out her glass.

Noreen nicely filled it, clearly mouthing the word devious.

The women returned to making the next day's assignment sheets.

"Well, that's it for me," Julie yawned after awhile. "I'm off to bed; big day tomorrow." The others nodded in agreement and cleaned up the table. The habits ingrained into them from childhood wouldn't allow them to leave a mess even if they were bone tired.

"Would you look at this?" Julie called as she looked out the window. They gathered at the front door in time to see Jessie and Millie getting out of the island's police car, its lights flashing.

"You don't suppose they got arrested for causing a disturbance, do you?" Noreen whispered.

"Thank you very much for the ride," Jessie said. "No, no, it won't be necessary to pick us up in the morning." The voice paused. "Yes, yes, of course I understand why you couldn't put on the siren, it's just that…"

"Mothers!" Deb said.

"Hide!" Pat added.

Looking up from the pile of papers strewn across his desk, Gary LeSeur glanced out the window, staring at the dark. Standing to stretch his aching back, he walked over to a table, and poured himself a cup. Looking at the murky sludge, he set it down and turned off the coffee pot.

"I'm getting too old for this," he said out loud to the empty office. He had looked through all the tedious reports of the day that came in during the time he had gone fishing: a cat in Ms. Olsen's tree (again), five traffic tickets, (you go Joe – with the income from tickets, we'll keep the lights on in this town yet); and old Otis being put into the tank (again).

He started to go over his notes on the ferry case, picking up a report from the Coast Guard. It said that they had gone through the bay and found nothing. They would wait for more information from him. There were several interviews with the ferry employees, and some with folks on the docks.

Not much, he realized. *How can I look for a suspect if I don't even know if there's a victim? Should I just stop the investigation right now, or not?* He sighed. *If Mike wasn't such a good friend… no,* he decided, *I'll give it forty-eight hours and if nothing turns up, I'll put it aside pending more information.*

Checking his watch, he stood once more. *Too late to call Deb on the island tonight to see if she has anything. I'll try her in the morning.* Turning off the light, he walked out to the empty parking lot and drove home.

Chapter Sixteen
June 22

"Holy moley, would you look at this!" Pat stood in her pajamas by the window, holding the curtain aside. Deb came up beside her, already dressed in her warm up suit.

"Is someone giving free food out there?" she asked, peering out over her friend's shoulder. Then, reality suddenly dawned. "They can't all be out there for the Tai Chi, can they?"

"Either that, or there's northern lights out there in the morning sky," Pat joked. "Well, better get on my clothes," she added, letting the curtain fall. "Good thing you've got Julie to help lead. You'll be fine."

"There are about a hundred women out in the street waiting for Tai Chi," Pat called to Noreen as she hurried to get dressed. "You'd best get a move on."

They heard a banging of the front door and without waiting for someone to open it, Julie walked in.

"I thought you said it would be a small crowd. What do you think is a big crowd? I've got someone out there setting up a portable mike system if you can believe it. We're probably going to need it. Are we ready?" she asked, turning to Deb.

"Not on your life, or rather on my life. You are leading the Italian version, *Pie Chi,* right?"

"Right. Sure. Don't worry, be happy. I even have some old Frank Sinatra tunes playing to get them in the mood."

Deb took a deep cleansing breath.

"Let's do it," she said. "Bye, all. We're leaving," Deb called to the others, with as much enthusiasm as she could muster. She and Julie headed out the door.

Strains of *When the Moon Hits Your Eye Like a Big Pizza Pie, That's Amore* wafted across the street as women and children started to warm up and position themselves for the morning opening. The sun was up and shining, quickly warming the gathering. An enterprising Lotta had set up a small stand nearby and was selling fresh coffee.

Julie walked briskly to the front of the group, pulling Deb with her. She picked up the mic.

"Welcome, it's so good to have you all here for 'Pie' chi. You'll find out what that means in a minute, but before we start, one of the organizers of the retreat has an announcement about a missing woman.

Deb took the mic.

"Hello. Quiet down, please. We're so glad you're out here this morning for this special event. We, law enforcement that is, are asking that if anyone knows of a woman that might be missing from your group, or from the retreat, to please contact Detective Gary LeSeur in the Ashland police department, or post it on the message board at Lotta's. She was last seen getting on the ferry two days ago from La Pointe. Please let us know if you have any information at all. Thank you." She handed the mic back to Julie.

Looking down, Deb saw that she had received a call from Gary. After pressing redial, he picked up on the first ring.

"So, you got anything for me?" Gary said into the phone. "Hey, turn down that radio will ya, I can't hear you."

Moving down the street away from the commotion, she tried again.

"It's our morning exercise, Gary, and good morning to you, too. You know I have more to do than be your detective."

"To Sinatra? Well, well. How the worm has turned. Seems you were always willing to poke your nose into my investigations before." Taking a deep breath, he reminded himself of what his wife had just told him that morning. 'Use honey,' she had said. 'Bullying is not the way to get information.'

"Sorry," he said. "I'm just tired, and I'm hoping you've found something."

"Forgiven. And I'm sorry, too. I meant to call you before because I might have something. Something I learned when I was getting a massage..."

"Really?" he interrupted. "Working hard, are we?"

"Detective LeSeur! Anyway, I was taking a break and getting a massage, and there was this woman getting one next to me"

"Jeeze, you women get massages in the same room?"

"Get past it bucko, and focus. Anyway, this woman..."

"What was her name?"

"Name? I can't remember, but anyway she seems to think the woman next door is missing, and that her husband, who the neighbor's been sleeping with, might have done something."

"Tell me more." Gary's voice became more interested.

Deb continued filling him in, while leaving out the part of the rocks rolling around the floor. None of his business anyway.

"Thanks for the information," Gary signed off. "I'll check on it."

"You're welcome. Bye."

Deb got in line to do Pie Chi, with strains of *When I Was Seventeen,* wafting through the air.

As Julie began to clear an area to prepare for the class to begin, Carolyn confidently eased her way into position. She turned to a woman next to her.

"Brr... I'm glad I brought a sweater with me. It's really cold."

"Nice sweater," the woman replied.

"Thank you. I got it at Benetton's in Maui on my last trip. My husband and I have a condo there. We go there every winter for a few months to escape the snow."

The woman shivered and pulled her well-worn blouse closer. Carolyn stomped her feet to warm herself.

"I just love being able to travel to warm places. We usually go to Maui and then Arizona," she continued.

The woman coughed.

Carolyn stopped stomping and looked at the woman as though seeing her for the first time, examining her closely.

My God, this woman must be my age and she looks really old.

"How nice for you that you have so many blessings in your life," the woman said sweetly.

Carolyn started at the woman's words, as though stung by them. At that moment, she felt a soft breeze on her face and was reminded of the journal entry.

"You know, I am blessed," she said, "but I don't think it's my stuff.. and by reminding me, you're a blessing to me." Pausing, she unbuttoned her sweater, removed it, and handed it to the woman. The woman hesitated, looked at Carolyn and saw her nodding encouragement. She took the sweater and put it on. Carolyn turned and began to button it for her.

"Thank you," the woman said with tears in her eyes.

"No. I owe you a big thanks," Carolyn replied, tears welling in her own eyes. After a quick hug, they both turned to the stage as the class began.

Deb turned to look out at the crowd, while squinting into the morning sunlight. *What would bring all these women out here?* she thought. *I know exactly why. It's the same reason we used to drag our kids out and meet our friends for Yoga and Tai Chi. No matter the craziness in my life back then, it meant so much to me to be able to escape and get energized and relaxed for a few hours. And it still means a lot.*

"Good morning, again. How many have done Tai Chi before?" Julie asked. Her smile radiated out at the crowd as many hands were raised. "For those of you who haven't, let me start with a simple explanation. Tai Chi was developed in ancient China as a martial art and is sometimes described as 'meditation in motion.' It promotes serenity through gentle movements – connecting the mind and body for stress reduction and to help with a variety of other health conditions. Well, guess what? We're not going to do it the man's way. Today we're going to do it a woman's way, and since I'm Italian, we're doing it in the style of old Italy. You could tell by the music, right?" There was a roar of laughter. "We're not going to use symbols of war or strife, but instead, today, we're going to make pizza."

The crowd laughed again, and Deb knew by watching that Julie had them in the palm of her hand.

"So let's begin. Let's start with some centering breaths... Breathe in and imagine the smell of fresh marinara sauce."

As Deb took her first deep breath and let it out, she looked around and marveled at the scene.

It's working. It's going to be okay.

As if the lake had heard her, a cooling breath of a breeze arose around the crowd.

Julie expertly led the women through the movements that followed.

"Now, let's do our warm-up. Just follow along. Twisty step left. Twisty step right."

"We'll just pretend to do some of the things we women do. Take your right hand and reach out and pretend to pick up a rag from the hook. Now, wipe the imaginary glass... lean... lean... lean... lean over and get the corner of that window," she said, gesturing to an imaginary window with her hand.

"Come on up here, girls," she called to three little girls in the front row. "I need your help to show these women how to do this." The three tots enthusiastically followed Julie's motions.

"First, we're going to pat the dog. Nice dog... pat, pat. Next, we'll pick up a bowl of food and feed the dog. There you go, doggie, here's your food, oh, look, you dropped some dog food on the floor. Scoop it up and put it in the dish."

"Since we have these beautiful long-haired girls here, let's pretend to part the girl's hair... and now, let's braid the girl's mane. Very good, everyone."

"Now, before we make our pizza, let's do a little dreaming. Stretch your arms way up over your head, like this," she continued. "Now, pull the window shade down. Good job."

"Now that we're done stretching, let's begin to make the pizza. That's right, we'll start by making the dough. Roll it out, roll it out... now spread the sauce. Let's finish by shaking the cheese... put the dough into the oven. Don't forget to take a deep breath and take in that delicious smell of fresh bread baking and garlic. Ooh... that's it, you've got it! Now, shall we try it all again?"

"Now we'll go into overtime and end by serving the pizza while holding back the pup," Julie said grandly, as she held her outstretched hand face-up directly in front of her while holding her right hand curled backwards next to her right hip.

"Wow, that was fun," Noreen said, wiping her face with a small hand towel. "But quite a workout." She and Carolyn were headed toward the coffee line where they saw Pat already drinking a cup. "Hey, how did you get yours first? Did you skip out early?"

"I left at the part about putting it in overtime," Pat answered. "If I had stayed, I would have had to find a pizza to eat afterwards. My body can't take the calories. Speaking of calories, let's get to Lotta's before every table is filled. The church called and said they had enough help."

Deb walked with Julie, who was surrounded by groupies.

"Great job. Rendezvous at Lotta's, okay?" Pat called out to them as they walked across the street toward her.

The day is going to be alright after all, she thought. She hurried to the cafe. *It will be a good place to ask questions about that missing woman. I've got to remember to check the message board.*

Chapter Seventeen
June 22

"I've got to hand it to you. You make a great breakfast. Where's this bread from? It's wonderful."

"Oh, I get it from Coco's in Washburn. She used to be an islander you know, and we islanders stick together."

"Well, it's great," Pat said between bites. "Got a minute?" she asked pulling out a chair and patting it.

Looking around, Lotta nodded.

"I guess. Just a minute though. Hey Jill, I'm taking a break, cover the front, will yah?" she called out toward the swinging doors on the kitchen.

"Right boss," a voice answered.

"So what's up, besides chaos?" Lotta asked as she sat down with Pat.

"Funny woman. First, thanks a lot for all you've done. But I was thinking; people are always telling you things."

"Don'tcha just know it! Yesterday this woman came in and..."

"Right...," Pat interrupted. "What I'm wondering about is whether anyone has said anything about the missing woman."

Lotta paused and thought for a moment.

"Truth is, lots of people have been talking about it in passing, but no one has said they know of a specific woman missing. But hey, I had one woman who thought your writing class today should be titled *Whatever Happened to the Missing Woman?*"

"Good idea." Pat laughed.

"Hey, Lotta! Can you come in here?" a voice called from the kitchen.

"Sounds like I better get in there," Lotta said as she stood up uneasily. "Oh, and Pat? Deb called and said to remind you to check the message board. And one more thing," she said, looking over her shoulder. "I still want to talk to you and Deb sometime when there's no one else around."

Modern technology. I can't hide from it, Pat thought.

Everywhere on the island, women were laughing, talking, and working together. Having once given themselves to getting away, they lost no time getting into the mood and fun of the crazy retreat.

"Hi, my name is Josie, I'm from Houston. And you are?"

"Really? You're from South Dakota, too? What a small world."

Greetings went round and round and women, who might have never been bold enough to speak to each other ordinarily, were having coffee together and, of course, discussing their families. The island seemed to have drawn them all together for the event, and the ambiance of natural beauty was encouraging them to enjoy themselves. It was as if the retreat now had a life of its own, and it was good. If there was a word or two of criticism for the chaos of the event, it was more than overcome by the overwhelming feeling of joy about attending a happening that no one would soon forget.

It had been a long morning and Pat and Carolyn took advantage of their break. They were walking down Main Street to stretch their legs when they heard the strains of guitar music.

"I think that's coming from the Beach House," Carolyn said. "Come on, Pat. Pick up the pace. Let's go see who's playing." Tugging on a reluctant

Pat, Carolyn continued to urge her along. "Isn't it you that says we should welcome opportunities as they come?"

My relatives walked down this street, Carolyn thought. *They might have come to enjoy a musician in a place like this, enjoying the free music and perhaps spending what little they had on a cup of coffee,* she mused as she came upon the outdoor patio.

I can't believe someone might not have enough to buy a simple cup of coffee. I just hope if they couldn't afford it, someone was nice enough to buy them one. When was the last time I noticed people enough that I knew to offer a cup of coffee to them?

"Come on Pat, I'll buy you an espresso. This is a moment to say yes to music, not work! Besides, someone might know something about the woman." She pulled Pat down the steps to where the music was wafting up from the fire pit area.

"You're right, Carolyn. Let's do it. Thanks for offering to buy. I'll get some chairs if you get the Joe."

"I can't explain it. I just feel so alive today. More than I can ever remember. Maybe next year, I'll buy for everyone!"

As Carolyn hurried off for the coffees, Pat nodded at two women who sat listening and tapping their feet. She was quickly swept away in the old folk song, *Those Were The Days*. Without realizing it, she started to softly harmonize with the singer.

From first childhood memories, Pat felt fed by all kinds of music: from the piano her sister practiced each day, to the sound of the wind through the birches, to the wild call of the crows.

Her sister recognized her hunger early on. "Wash my dishes for me tonight," she bartered, "and I'll play *Moonlight Sonata* while you work. *A bargain,* thought little Patty, whose hands were in hot soapy water, but whose soul was in the sky.

Now, enjoying the sun and the song, Pat didn't realize at first that she was being watched by an amused Native woman. When Pat eventually noticed her, the woman smiled back.

"Go up and sing with her," she whispered encouragingly. Startled by the support, Pat started to shake her head no, but then remembered what Carolyn had said.

Why the heck not? she thought. She got up from her chair.

Minutes later, Carolyn returned to hear Pat's familiar voice singing harmony with a local singer. She placed the cup beside her friend on the ledge of the fire pit and settled in to listen.

So this is what living in the moment means, she thought happily. *I'm going to try it more often. I'm going to call Tom and tell him about this.*

The harmonies floated on the crisp lake air of the bay as she pulled out her cell and sent him a text instead.

Wow, I've got to remember to tell Pat to publish her songs, she thought, losing herself in the music.

Endings and Beginnings

When I was a girl, life was always beginning.
New starts, new stories, new shoots from the root.
Always beginning when I was a youngling,
Life was a spark I thought always would glow.

Life is beginnings, the start of a new bud,
The egg becomes bird, and the bud a sweet fruit.
But the wind keeps us moving to places unknowing,
Like seasons we keep changing, the changeling her suit.

When I was a young woman my life breath was strong,
Beginnings continued like lines in a song.
A life full of beginning, strength without end
The sparks would keep coming, always my friend.

Then endings began, one first, then another,
You can name them yourself, if you have been me.
And then I thought it would always be endings,
Nothing ever new, nothing ever free.

But endings are temporary or so I am learning,
Arms round each other we sit here again.
The wind once again it seems to be turning.
The spring always comes as my mother once said.

The spring always comes and with it now sunshine,
The bird on the tree, life rising from earth.
So sing the song softly, a woman's song sweetly,
But sing it most strongly because it's rebirth.

A round of applause drew Pat from her song. Looking up, she noticed Carolyn smiling and waving her cup.

"Thanks for letting me sing," she said to the guitarist.

"You're most surely welcome anytime. See you at the bonfire tonight. Let's sing it again there, okay?"

Winding her way through the tables, Pat was startled to see that her chair was taken by a man. He was engaged in an animated conversation with Carolyn.

"Oh, Pat," Carolyn said, as she gave her a high five. She appeared flustered, as if caught at something.

"This is...," her voice trailed off. When he was not forthcoming, she continued. "Anyway he has a cottage here, and he lives in it six months of the year. Can you believe it?"

Pat turned to the big man whose wide smile showed gleaming TV white teeth. His two-hundred-dollar hair cut was unmessed by the winds; the sides of his hair had just a touch of grey.

Charmer, she thought.

"Not really a cottage; it's more like a house. Great song, by the way. Was that an old Joni Mitchell?"

"Nope, it's an old one of mine, actually. Hi, I'm Pat," she said, holding out her hand. "So, you're an islander?"

"No, not really. We go to the West Indies in the winter. Hey, barkeep, a drink for the lovely ladies. Lets make it that drink of the weekend I heard so much about, a cup of 'Witches Brew' for everyone."

The waitress studiously kept her face straight, but glanced at Pat knowingly.

Everyone has met men like this before, Pat thought.

"Ever tried Maui? We have a condo there. It's great," Carolyn said.

He turned slowly and looked at her with renewed interest. "Yes, yes we have, but the crowds... So, you own there, on the beach?"

"Oh, yes. Of course, we rent it out when we're not there."

"We? I take it then, pretty lady, you are attached?"

"What?" a flustered Carolyn replied. "Yes, of course."

"Me, too," he said with a sigh. Turning to the waiter who was now standing with a bill, he waved his hand dismissively.

"Put it on my wife's tab."

"Where is your house, may I ask?" Pat inquired, as something niggled in the back of her mind.

"Over down Nebraska Row. Perhaps you would like to come for cocktails while you're here?"

"That would have been great, really," Carolyn jumped in before Pat could answer. "Maybe another time. We're so busy with the retreat, you know. Is your wife currently here?" she asked pointedly.

He stared into her eyes and then shifted them slightly down.

"Yes, yes. She had a great hot rock massage at Lotta's yesterday, thanks to the masseuse you brought in. Well, I mustn't take up anymore of your time. Ciao." He walked away, looking for all the world like a snake hunting a nice fat mouse.

"Do you think that was a toupee?" Carolyn asked. They laughed together. "You've still got a great voice, girl. But wait until you hear what I heard in the bathroom!"

"You were eavesdropping on women in the stalls?" Pat asked, pretending to be shocked.

"Worse," Carolyn said, leaning in conspiratorially. "I was listening to guys in the men's toilet. It's a common wall, and they were loud," she added when she saw the surprised look on Pat's face.

"Spill it. Even though I don't like eavesdropping, what the heck, the damage is already done."

"Well, of course I don't know who they were. They didn't use names or anything, but two men were, you know, peeing and…"

"No physical details, please. Just get on with it."

"One was talking about his girlfriend, or ex, I suppose, because she had left him, you see, or at least that's what he said, but Pat, what if she didn't leave, but was the one on the ferry? And he, you know…"

"Slow down. Start over... from the beginning," Pat added, "except not the urinal part, please."

"Well, like I said, this one guy was sort of bragging about getting rid of his girlfriend. That's his exact words. *'I got rid of her,'* he said. I couldn't quite catch what the other guy said, some darn woman flushed, but it was sort of like he thought the woman had dropped him. He was cynical-like. Then, the first guy got real loud, and I didn't have to try to listen at all. 'Hell, no,' he said. 'That bitch was in my life too long, wanted me to change everything, and complained about everything. Finally, two days ago, we had this big fight, and I told her to get out.' Then the other guy laughed and said, 'more like she *walked out* you mean.'"

"What happened next?"

"Well, they must have left. I washed my hands, and went out hoping I could see who they were. And there they were sitting at the bar. I recognized their voices. Boy, did I go by fast."

"Would you recognize them again?"

"You mean in a line up or something? Sure. At least I think so. One was a big lumberjack kind of guy, sort of like my second husband, you know with long dark hair? And the other was older, a little weasel with a fat mustache. But here's the thing... do you think he followed her onto the ferry and you know?" She made a pushing motion with her hands.

"Good work, Nancy Drew. We'll call Gary and tell him. Got your cell?" She punched in the number she really shouldn't remember by heart, but did.

"Just remind me never to tell secrets when you are in the next room," she teased.

"LeSeur here."

She took a deep breath and started to explain quickly before he could hang up.

Chapter Eighteen
June 22

"Ladies! I hope you've been having a great morning. Listen up! I have a surprise for you!" Deb hollered into the megaphone at the crowded street. Some of the women paused from their gabbing and turned to look at Deb. "We will gather at the beach across from the church at twelve thirty for a group photo. Everyone should come." A few women clapped.

"This is an historic event, and you don't want to be left out." Deb noticed some women shrugging and turning away. She felt that she had to give one more plea. "You know, my friends and I always took photos of ourselves on retreats, and those photos are some of my favorite photos in my album. What I regret is the people who chose not to be in the pictures. Remember, this is your retreat. Tell all your friends!" Her challenge seemed to rally the women as word was quickly passed further and further through the town. Soon, groups were hastening toward the beautiful little beach, dragging all the materials from workshops with them.

"Pictures?" Pat overheard as she arrived on the scene. "Look at my hair! Does anyone have a brush?"

With all the watercolor paint on her blouse and no makeup at all, the woman looked more like a troll than a matriarch.

"Anyone have any wipes?" a voice asked.

"I have to go change. Wait for me!" another called.

Deb felt amused as she looked around at the happy crowd of disheveled women.

What am I thinking? she thought, as she looked down at her shirt in dismay. *I can't be in a picture with a coffee stain down my front.*

Earlier in the day, Deb had been convinced by Linda that the gathering was an event worth photographing. It was something Deb had not planned for, but Linda had volunteered to take the pictures.

"A simple thing," Linda had said. "A row of women seated, a row behind on their knees, a row seated in chairs, and a row standing in the back. And if any women are left over we can have them lying on beach towels in the front."

So like Linda to be organized, Deb thought, grateful for the well-thought-out plan. *I wouldn't mind having a photo of this gathering, if I can get Gracie to stand still long enough.*

She spotted her daughter and granddaughter in the crowd.

Jeeze, where's my mother?

As the women gathered on the beachfront, Deb stared at the crowd. It dawned on her that things weren't going the way Linda planned.

For one thing, there are so many women and children. How will we ever get everyone to stand still?

Linda had managed to escape the whole beach scene by convincing Detective LeSeur to take her out into the lake in his fishing boat in order to get the best possible photo.

Leave it to cute Linda to still be able to wrap men around her finger, Deb thought enviously. Linda stood without a life vest, precariously balancing between two seats in the boat as the waves gently rocked her back and forth.

Now there's a picture I wish I had, Deb thought.

"Careful there, Missy," Gary said.

Deb stood on the beach with her megaphone, trying to navigate through the crowds and separate the women into lines.

This is like herding cats, she thought. The crowd was happy and excited but more interested in gossiping than in organizing into rows that would take them even temporarily away from newfound friends. Some of the women climbed atop the wooden lifeguard stand, posing off the sides as though they were firefighters on a truck.

No one seemed to be listening or paying the least bit of attention to Deb's entreaties.

Take a deep breath, Deb thought as she glanced around the crowd, looking for help.

She noticed Bev navigating her electric cart expertly over the rocks and onto the beach, determined to enter into the fray. Noreen and Julie sat together on the park bench, Noreen with paint on her cheek and Julie twirling a croquet mallet.

At least Carolyn is helping. Where is Pat, anyway? Deb thought.

Carolyn was doing her best to help recruit volunteers to get chairs from the church across the street.

"Follow me, ladies. We need chairs for this photo to work.

"What? We're on a retreat!" a middle-aged brunette called out from the crowd. "You can't really expect us to carry chairs out here! You've got to be kidding!"

Carolyn glanced at Deb and threw her arms in the air in a determined pose.

"Yes, everyone has to help," she called out in her teacher voice.

Looking sheepish, the women followed her into the church.

I sure am glad I have friends, Deb thought. *The thought was soothing to her.*

"Hurry up! It's rough out here in this boat!" Linda called faintly from her perch in the waves offshore.

"Line 'em up! I've got to get fishing!" LeSeur's voice boomed out authoritatively. "Careful, there," he said to Linda. "I don't want to fish you out of the drink."

Time to be bold, Deb thought.

She elbowed her way through the crowd and climbed up on the lifeguard stand.

"Please move away from the stand! We've got a picture to take!" she said to the women hanging off the sides.

"Here, Deb!" Millie called. "We want you to stand by us!"

"Do you have a wide angle lens?" Carolyn called out to Linda. "We always use a wide angle lens when we're in Maui!"

"I can't hear what she's yelling!" Linda called back from the boat.

"Okay, ladies! Here's the deal," Deb bellowed into the megaphone. "We're going to get a picture. And we don't want one of your back ends!

So face the lake and that lady with the camera out there in the boat. On the count of three, I'll say cheese and you all smile! Ready. One, two, three. Pizza! She held her fingers high in the air as she counted. Despite her best efforts, the picture still had backsides in it.

At the moment Deb said pizza, a large black crow flew right into the frame of the picture.

"We have to do another one!" Linda yelled, her legs wobbling on the seats. "This time without the crow!"

Six takes later, Linda was still not satisfied, but Deb had a mutiny on her hands and Gary was threatening to start the motor.

"That's it! We're done!" Deb bellowed out to the boat. "Cut! Done! Finito. No more!"

"Be free, ladies! You are released from captivity," she yelled to the crowd. A cheer arose from the gathering.

"Oh, good," a voice called. "I wanted to be sure I got to the next class on time. Anybody know where I can get some of those fish livers?"

Deb climbed down from the lifeguard chair just in time to meet Linda at the shoreline being gingerly helped from the boat by a very impatient appearing Detective LeSeur. Looking at his watch, he turned toward Deb.

"You owe me... get me a list by tonight." Pulling at his motor cord, he expertly maneuvered his boat into the waves and sped out into the vast lake. He didn't even wave back at Deb's goodbye.

I'm glad my husband doesn't act like that, Linda thought, with a self-satisfied look.

"Did you get a good one?" Deb asked eagerly as the crowd of women began to scatter in several directions.

"I'm sure I did, but I nearly went into the drink trying. And that's not the least of it. When I went down to the beach to find a boat, that cute police officer with Gary tried to invite me to spend the day on the lake with him. But I wasn't interested in fishing!"

"Neither was he," Deb replied. "Let's see the photos!" She tried not to laugh when she realized that in all the pictures, the women looked like pinheads, not recognizable to anyone else but themselves. As she rescanned through the digital images, Deb stopped at the last one.

"This is probably the best one of all of them," she said, looking closer.

"Look at this, will you?" She pointed to the blurry image of a woman who, unlike all the others, appeared to have light reflecting on her face. The woman was resting a hand on a dog's head. Her hand also reflected light.

"Do we know this woman?" Deb asked, recognizing the dog. "Maybe the dog belongs to her."

"I haven't seen her before," Linda replied. "But then again, with all these people here, I couldn't begin to tell you who I've seen and who I haven't!"

"Maybe the historical society would like one of these pictures," Carolyn suggested.

Ignoring Carolyn, Linda grabbed the megaphone from Deb's hand.

"Ladies! Ladies! I just want everyone to know that I will make a complimentary photo for each of you! All you have to do is get me your name and address on a piece of paper, and I'll take care of getting it to you."

A murmur arose from the dispersing crowd.

"Really? That's really nice."

"Just bring your names to me at the..."

She paused.

"Wait a minute! What am I doing?" Linda muttered under her breath. "I can't believe I just said that."

Putting the megaphone back to her mouth, she yelled, "Sorry about this, ladies, but disregard what I just said... I will put a post on Lotta's bulletin board of an on-line cite where you can order a photo if you choose."

"Whew!" Pat said. "That was a close call."

"I'm learning," Linda replied.

"Good for you," Pat said.

"Well, I'm off to put photos online. What are you going to do now?"

"Hey, Pat, let's go for a ride out in the woods. I need a chance to clear my head," Deb called out just then as Pat helped the others stack chairs to return to the church.

"Sounds good," Pat replied. "Let's finish here, first, and then let's stop by Tommy's and grab something. I haven't had lunch yet."

Eager for some lunch, Pat didn't notice the skinny guy until he was almost upon her. Standing toe to toe with her, whiskey on his breath, he raised his fist, and Pat drew back in alarm.

"Are you the ones?" You're the ones, aren't you?" he taunted. "The ones who have been gossiping about me."

"What?" Pat asked. Then she got mad. "Who the hell are you, and what are you talking about?" She took a step forward.

"I heard you were spreading rumors about me and my girlfriend. Do you make it a practice to listen to guys in men's toilets?"

This is the weasel Carolyn heard, Deb thought, stepping between Pat and the man.

"Why would you care anyway, unless she's really disappeared?" Deb asked. "Answer this: Where is she?"

He backed up, confused.

"It's just that we had a fight, and she left." He started to turn to leave. "Stay out of my business," he said, turning his head towards her. And he left.

"So that's the guy," Deb said. "We'll add him to our list of suspects."

"Come on, buddy, let's go get lunch," Pat said.

Chapter Nineteen
June 22

Not all the retreaters felt the need to go to workshops. Some thought it was a higher calling to go to the beach. Greasy with suntan oil and fortified with ice tea, beach blankets, and books, they allowed the lake to draw them. Some of these women were even members of Pat's own family. Go figure.

"Wake up, grandma, wake up." Jessie was suddenly startled from her afternoon nap in the sun by a small stick poking her in the side.

"Huh? Oh, yes, Willow dear. I'm awake. See, my eyes are open."

"No, you're not." Willow looked closely, stomping her little foot in the sand. "No, you're not! You haven't seen the world I've been making." She pointed with her stick to the mounds of sand where she had been digging.

"How lovely dear. What is it?"

"If you were really awake you, would know." Relenting, Willow continued. "Its okay, Grandma. I'll show you. This is my house," she said in her sing song voice as she pointed. "This is Skylar's house, and this one way over here is Grandma Pat's. You can stay with her," she explained.

"Where is your little brother's house?" Jessie asked gently, knowing that the new interloper was a sore point for Willow.

"Oh, he just comes to visit. This is girl town. If you want to come, you have to STAY AWAKE!" she said, noticing her great-grandmother's drooping eyelids.

Staying awake, Jessie thought, *how much of my life have I chosen to sleep away? But no more,* she thought resolutely. *What time I have left I'm going to spend awake.*

She settled back in the comfortable Adirondack chair.

"A lot can happen when you let yourself go to sleep," Willow said sternly, looking up from her digging.

Out of the mouths of babes, Jessie thought. *But you, my little darling, I'm betting that you will stay awake through it all.* She sent the thought up to whatever beneficent spirit was watching.

All around the white-haired matriarch and the blonde little girl, women were laughing and splashing in the lake.

"This was a great idea," Deb said, as she looked around. "Would you look at these signs? *Let's Make Getting into Trouble Fun Again,*" she read aloud. *"If you can't dazzle 'em with brilliance, baffle 'em with bullshit.* I've forgotten what a riot this place is."

"Yup, the Burned Down Café is one of a kind, alright," Pat answered. "No, thanks, one's enough for me," she said, putting up the front of her hand toward the bartender. "How's the bar business been with all us women here?"

"It's great being crazy busy, but it must be the full moon," he said wiping up the bar next to them.

"What's been happening?" Deb asked.

"Oh, you know... crazy stuff. Right before you came in there were some mainlanders in having drinks. One guy asked for a martini right here, can you imagine? So I made him one, and then he complains. 'Is this Stoli's gin in this martini? I only drink Stoli's.' Where does he think he is, anyway? Look around you. This is a tent, for goodness sake! Our drink of choice is Heinies. Typical non-islanders."

He leaned forward on the bar.

"The guy came in here with big dreams. He was trying to impress the woman he was with. First thing he does is light a cigarette. I told him he couldn't smoke in here. He told me how he had investors just waiting to build some kind of huge fun land resort like the Wisconsin Dells, right here. When the woman was skeptical about where he would get enough land, he said he had a plan to get it from the east side."

"The east side!" Now Deb wasn't just pretending to be interested in what he had to say. "Isn't that the Native land?"

"Yup, can you believe it? Evidently, he picked the wrong woman to impress. When she got mad and said she wouldn't let it happen, she would make sure of it, he got real quiet-like, and said something like, 'nobody gets in my way.' Then he stood up and raised his fist menacingly at the woman. Just like that. Tell you what, that guy gave me the creeps. I was just about to reach under the bar for my handy deterrent."

He lifted up a baseball bat for them to see.

"I think the woman took him seriously. She stood up and said, 'I won't tell, really,' and then she left in a hurry. And the guy? He followed her out." Shaking his head, he turned to get a beer for another customer. "And he didn't even leave a tip. That was a frickin' mistake. See if he ever gets a martini here again. Like I said, it must be the full moon."

Deb nodded her head in agreement, and then turned to Pat.

"Do you think this one could be the missing woman?"

"Don't know. Let's just take a little drive up the road and see how we feel about it after a walk in the woods. If we decide it's important, we'll call Gary. Remember, we have to be back for the writing workshop before three."

Chapter Twenty
June 22

There is something about encountering evil, no matter the form, that makes one want to forget. Afterwards, Deb didn't want to remember this walk in the woods with Pat. Her reticence remained, despite her knowledge that it is better not to forget such encounters, in order to be better prepared to fight.

It all started out ordinarily enough, as do most such encounters. Before getting out of the car, Deb glanced at the clock. It was one-thirty.

Plenty of time, she thought. Looking around to try to get her bearings, she took in the intrinsic beauty of the wild island. The sun was shining almost straight down, lighting the leaves and branches on its way to warm the earth.

Great time for a walk, she thought.

What was that? She paused and sniffed. Something was in the air. A smell. *Not a smoke smell... no, not exactly a scent, but something more. Usually I can walk all of Madeline without a fear, but now, it's as though the sun isn't reaching me.* She shivered, noticing the shadows on the ground, at the same time the sun shone above.

Closing the car door, she turned to her friend.

"Where are we? How could we possibly get lost on Madeline Island?" Deb shook her head. "We've been coming here for years. And the truth is, I don't remember this road at all." She glanced around, trying once again to get her bearings, and hoping to find a sign displaying the words, "Go This

Way, Sillies." It didn't happen.

"Like we have to *try* to get lost." It was a standing joke that traveling together anywhere might lead them to end up in Canada. Deb locked the door and stretched.

"Let's walk back to the last road sign. I'm tired of being in the darn car."

"Road sign? Isn't that why your hubby bought you that shiny new box?" Marc had tired of the women complaining about being lost, and had bought her a G.P.S. for Christmas.

"Fat lot of good that thing is doing. It's as if we're in the Bermuda triangle." She got serious for a moment. "Do you feel it?"

"You mean that cold?" Pat responded, walking beside Deb. "I thought it was just my imagination. I wish we were back in town. What's with this place?"

Looking uneasily at the woods on both sides of them, Deb started walking down the center of the dirt road, rather than by the edge. Maybe it was silly, but she couldn't help herself. Pat walked right next to her, not wanting to be left behind.

"You know what it reminds me of? It reminds me of the woods Dorothy and her crew went through when they were seeking the wicked witch."

"Oh, that makes me feel so much better."

Coming upon the sign, Pat reached up and brushed off the dirt covering its face. Instead of a direction, it read, Dead End.

"Well, that's informative." She looked up at the sky, searching for the sunlight. There were no clouds above them, and yet, here in the dense woods, it was positively gloomy.

They stood close, instinctively knowing it was safer that way. Safer from what, they couldn't say. Their arms touched as their eyes adjusted to the gloom.

Watching the light from above, she followed it with her eyes as it filtered down catching on the tips of leaves, trickling through as if trying to reach them.

Pat stood listening so hard that she unconsciously held her breath. They stood like two frozen statues.

What am I listening for? she wondered. Her heart beat as fast as a sparrow caught in a cage.

CAW! CAW!

"Snap!" Deb said, startled out of the invisible spell by the sound of a gigantic blue-black crow that landed right in front of them. "What's she got there?" she asked curiously, as she leaned toward the bird, still holding onto Pat's arm,

Pat moved a step closer to get a better look, her ill feeling dispelled some by her friend's use of the silly child's swear word. The magnificent bird seemed to look right into Pat's eyes and had landed on the carcass of a porcupine. As they watched, fascinated and appalled, it casually ripped off a piece. Throwing it up it the air, it caught the meat and swallowed.

"Shoo." Deb gestured with her arms to scare it away. Pat stopped her before the motion was complete.

"It means no harm. But where are the other birds?" she whispered. "We should be hearing birds. Something here has scared them away."

She squinted, and an involuntary shiver went through her.

"What is it?" Deb asked. "What do you see?"

Pat shook her head.

"Nothing, I guess. For a moment, I could have sworn I saw a form... an outline of someone standing just out of range. I suppose it could have been a birch tree. Their branches sometimes look like arms. It's nothing."

The crow cawed again, as if in warning. Taking Deb's arm, she slowly turned, easing them back down the road to the car. The new red shoes she was wearing were slick on the bottom, and she slipped, barely staying upright. She held onto Deb once again.

With one last CAW, the crow flew up and away. Then, silence.

"Deb, do you still carry that small flashlight on your key chain?"

"Yes," Deb answered as she fumbled around in her pocket. "Here it is."

A thin beam cut through the eerie fog, and a figure stepped casually into its light. They gasped. From their vantage point, they could see the silhouette of a man. The light showed an elegant figure with tangles of long black hair. They heard the flick of a lighter as the man cupped a hand to his face, bringing the flame to the end of his cigarette. He took his time to inhale before looking up with a smile that didn't even try to reach his eyes.

"Hello ladies. I've been expecting you." He calmly walked closer to them onto the road. The women stood frozen, clinging to each other.

Pat reacted without thinking.

"You scared the crap out of us! What the hell are you doing out here?" she barked in a hoarse voice. She had one hand in Deb's, the other held to her breast, trying to keep her heart from pounding right through her chest.

Funny what you can notice in an instant, she thought. *Designer slacks, Italian shoes, immaculate black shirt, rolled up sleeves showing off his tan. But it's his eyes! Such a handsome face. If cruel can be handsome.*

He smiled again, and the smoke curled out of his nose.

"I hope the crow didn't scare you too much."

Deb stared at him, like a deer caught for a moment in the headlights of a truck. Noticing that Deb was frozen, Pat kicked her. She couldn't even imagine what her empathic friend was feeling from what was rolling off of him. But now was not the time for empathy.

"Ouch," Deb said.

"Guard yourself," Pat whispered.

What did that Yoga master tell me about protecting myself? Deb thought. *Something about keeping my spirit safe by using the power of my thoughts...*

He took another long draw on the cigarette.

"Walk with me a while. You know you're curious. You know you want to." Pat realized that it was true. As much as she tried to live in the light, she wondered about the other side.

Who is this guy anyway, and what's he offering? Who does he think we are?

Now it was Deb's turn to kick.

"No. There must be some misunderstanding. Were you thinking you were meeting someone here? If you were, it's not us," Deb said. "We're not going anywhere with you."

"Aren't you the ones coming to talk about the land?" he asked, suddenly frowning and taking a step back.

Pat, realizing the mistake, looked at him more closely. "No... no, we're not," she said. "But aren't you the guy who had the fight in the bar with that woman? The bartender told us she disappeared afterwards."

"Disappeared? Or left by her own choice? Does it matter?" He sneered. "The question is who sent you?" He looked at them disdainfully.

"No one sent us," Pat said firmly.

"Sure! You mean you just came to see me on your own? You two must really be gullible. What are you here for, then? Just a little fling in the woods? A subplot for a new book? A story to write home to your husbands?" he taunted.

"As a matter of fact, we had no intention of meeting up with some stupid stranger on a beautiful day like this when we have so much work to do...," Deb blurted out, finding her voice.

"Shut up, Deb!" Pat said, elbowing her and motioning with her right index finger over her lips.

"In case you haven't noticed, it takes both halves of the wheel to make the wagon go around," the man said mysteriously. "Can't have one without the other. You know, no ying without yang. No up without down, no in without out..."

"And no light without the dark," Pat continued, looking the man directly in the face.

"You see, it's not so bad. I'm not that different from what you know. Nothing to be scared of is there, Ma'am? What did you say your name was?" the man asked coolly of Pat, extending his hand in mock greeting. "If you come with me, I can show you some things you've never seen before or even thought to dream of... something even better than your favorite dream of flying. It would even be better than winning the lottery every time you bought a ticket."

"Pat! Don't touch him!" Deb whispered, quickly noticing Pat's piqued interest in the man and grabbing her hand before Pat could extend it back.

"Get real, girlfriend! We're out in the woods," Deb continued. "Remember what we are trying to do here this weekend." Deb grew visibly frustrated at Pat's fixation on the man's eyes.

"Damn it! We're doing a retreat here, not solving a mystery with dangerous people."

Pat turned to Deb.

"I can save the island. I think this is the guy who wants to build a big fun-land on half of this place." Pat whispered.

"No, Pat.

Pat didn't back away, but she dropped her head.

"Well, I can see that we're not going anywhere today," the man sneered, letting his outstretched hand fall to his side. "I'm not wasting my time with you two."

Tipping his head, he flicked his cigarette butt on the road right by their feet. Looking at the two women through lidded eyes he slowly put it out with the heel of his shoe.

"Can't be too careful, you know. These woods are valuable."

Pat watched as he faded back into the woods. Looking quickly around them, the women took a deep breath and exhaled loudly.

"What was that all about?" Deb asked.

CAAW!

Swooping down, the crow landed with a skid on the gravel in front of them, almost embarrassed by her rough landing. Flapping her wings, she seemed in a hurry to move them along, an idea with which they hardily concurred. Ahead of them was the little Miata, the sun shining off its window. Hurrying to it, the women pulled open the doors, eager to leave.

Before settling in, Deb turned and slightly bowed to their winged friend, throwing the half eaten candy bar she had left on the seat.

"Thank you," she said solemnly. "Tell your lady we thank her too," she said, remembering her talk with the Native woman. "Well, that was a relaxing walk," Deb said, turning to Pat.

She turned the key, and time began again.

"Have a cookie," Deb said, handing a piece to Pat. "There's nothing like chocolate to soothe the savage beast."

"Then maybe we should have thrown some at that guy." Pat laughed nervously.

"What exactly happened back there?" Deb gunned her motor throwing up a train of dust behind them.

"I think we disturbed something he was doing, and he wanted to make sure we were gone in a hurry."

"Why do you say that?"

"Because if he was innocent, he would have stepped out, given us directions, and sent us on our way. No, he was guilty alright. I just don't know of what yet."

"It was sort of spooky."

"Come on, Deb."

"You know you felt it too!" Deb said accusingly. "Do you think it has anything to do with the missing woman?"

"Next, you'll be telling me he's buried her and ten others in the woods."

Deb shivered, clamping her hands more firmly on the wheel. "Don't even kid about it."

"You're right. There was something out there alright," Pat conceded. "I've felt it once or twice before."

"But now that I look back at it, he really was trying to get us out of there awfully fast. Was he meeting someone? Someone we might recognize? Who did he think sent us?"

"This is one, for sure, that we need to call Gary about," Deb said.

Turning into town she screeched to a halt as twenty or so women wandered across the road like a herd of deer right in front of the car.

"Lucy, we're back."

"I'm going first!" Pat called, after they returned to the cabin.

"No, let me," Deb insisted, playfully pushing her way to beat Pat to the shower.

They sat afterwards with their friends, before leaving for their workshop.

"Things just keep getting stranger and stranger," Deb said. "Why is it that the more I learn about something, the less I know about it?"

"What do you mean?" Linda asked.

"Yesterday, I was ready to dismiss the whole idea of a woman really disappearing from the ferry as far-fetched and hysterical imagining. Today, I am not so sure."

"So what happened today?"

"It just seems like everywhere we go we keep seeing possible clues about who the woman was," Pat said.

"And why it is plausible that someone would disappear," she added. "I'm just wondering if we have sown seeds of hysteria out here. Just talking it up all over the island could make everyone assume someone's missing, even if they're not."

"What are you talking about?" Julie asked.

"First, I met a woman while getting a massage who insisted the mystery woman was her husband's lover," Deb said.

"Then there was a guy at the bathroom at the Beach Club this morning," Carolyn interjected.

"You should have seen Pat go toe to toe with that guy," Deb said. "I think we met him on our way to lunch. What a guy! I thought he was going to hit Pat. And he didn't deny that his girlfriend was missing."

"Wow," Julie said. "This is just like one of your mysteries."

"We're locking our doors tonight." Carolyn said.

"The worst of all was the guy we met in the woods this afternoon," Pat said.

Deb listened distractedly.

What a couple of days! First, the story about the spirit protecting the island. Then, the creepy guy in the woods, she thought, feeling a chill on her neck at the memory. *I wonder if good really does conquer evil. Can I really depend on it?*

"It's like the universe is sending a message," Deb said, returning her attention to the room. "Pay attention. There are clues all around us if we choose to see them."

"Let she who has eyes, see," Pat added, adapting a biblical quote.

"There are some things in life that I'd rather not see," Deb continued. "Like the creep in the woods."

"I wonder if he's the same guy that Pat told us about while you were in the shower... the one the bartender told you about," Linda offered.

"I think we need to be careful about connecting imaginary dots here," Deb said, her legal mind taking over. "Remember, this is an island. While everything may appear to be connected, we can't jump to conclusions without more convincing proof. We don't want a bunch of frightened women, do we?"

"Anyway, it's not our job to figure this all out," Bev said.

"Guess it's time to call LeSeur," Deb agreed. She pulled out her cell.

"Halloooo, anyone home?" she heard from the direction of the door before she could dial.

"So, I heard about your class for the kids," Noreen called back as the two Moms walked into the kitchen. "It sounded great! I wish you had one for grownups."

Millie's face pinkened with pride as she looked around the table.

"So, what are you all talking about? You look so serious. Did one of your workshops go awry? At least we didn't serve liquor at ours," she said with a twinkle in her eye.

"Hey, I didn't serve it," Julie said. "They brought it themselves."

Pat shook her head.

"If only! No, we've just been talking about the missing woman."

"So they didn't find her yet?" Jessie asked, reaching for a glass.

"No. We've got some theories, but that all. It's just so frustrating. Deb's connecting with LeSeur right now."

"Sometimes, dear, we don't know all the answers. We just have to put it in God's hands," Millie said sympathetically.

"Please!" Pat said, before she could stop herself.

"Really," Jessie said. "It's just a way of talking." Taking a sip from her glass, she eyed her daughter. "Sometimes we do all we can and then, well, we just keep going."

"But I like to know."

"Don't we all, dearie? In my ninety-three years there were times when things just couldn't always be tied up with neat little bows. I learned it early. I was eight when my dad disappeared."

"Disappeared?"

"Yes, your grandfather... my father... who I loved with all my heart, went off to work at the track with the horses and just never came back. My mother was convinced he went back to Wales, and she burned all his things out on the lawn. What a bonfire that was with all the neighbors standing around. But we just never knew what happened."

"Never?"

"No. After a while it didn't really matter whether he was killed in a fight or went back to Wales. What mattered was that he was gone."

Millie patted Jessie's hand.

"I know what you mean. When I say leave it in God's hands, what I really mean is that this woman may have chosen just to leave. Face it, you never know. Life isn't neat. It's just… life."

"I still think it's possible the woman is not real at all," Pat said.

"Not real? How could she not be real when everyone's talking about her?" Carolyn asked. "What do you mean by that?"

"Just stay with me a moment," Pat answered. "I mean not real in the sense of being physically real. Maybe she is the Goddess of the island."

"What the heck are you talking about?" Carolyn asked.

"Lots of people have been talking about the spirit of the island," Pat answered.

"I have a little trouble with that," Carolyn replied. "After all, the woman left the boat."

"Even if it is a spirit, I'm a little uncomfortable calling her a Goddess," Linda said.

"Well," Millie said. "We've made God male for over two thousand years in the Bible. Remember, even in Genesis it says that both males and females were created in the image of God. I say it's about time we even it up."

"Maybe you're right," Linda said, reaching over and patting her hand.

They sat listening to Deb's voice in the background still talking on her cell.

"Spirit or not," Linda said, "the question is, did someone go off the boat? Before we give up on this mystery, let's at least see what we've got." She jumped up and reached for her charts of suspects and potential victims.

"We're with you, bippy. Lead on," Jessie said, raising her glass.

Millie and Jessie gave each other a knowing smile.

"You won't believe what I just learned," Deb said, returning to the room.

"What?" Pat asked.

"Gary just told me that Lotta has spent time in prison."

"That can't be! She's our friend."

"It's true."

"But she doesn't seem like the type," Carolyn said.

"We all have our secrets," Deb replied.

Chapter Twenty-One
June 22

"Welcome to the bonfire."

Deb stood before the women gathered around the unlit fire pit. "Pat, would you come up and join me please?" Leaving her spot between her two grandchildren, Pat stood up next to Deb.

"Here we are at the peak solstice hour," Deb began. "We gather around this fire to honor the ending of one season in our lives and to make space for a new beginning." She paused as the noise from the crowd settled down.

"Celebrating the solstice has been observed by many different traditions for thousands of..."

"Come, on, light my fire!" Jessie exclaimed. Other women murmured in agreement.

"Oh, Mother," Pat said under her breath.

"Jessie," Deb said, without missing a beat. "Your fire never goes out. You've always had a fire in your belly... towards life."

"Sure, sure," Jessie said, brushing Deb off. "I just meant that I want to get on with the dancing. Enough talking and the big words."

Deb smiled at the eagerness of a ninety-three-year old woman to engage in the dance.

"I know that people have had new beginnings this week. So, now we celebrate them all. Let the party begin!"

Reaching down, she struck a match and lit the kindling.

The flames from the big log fire shot up, causing the ring of women around the pit to lean back collectively and laugh. One woman, followed by another, picked up guitars from their cases and started to play. The music was wild, gypsy sounding, almost making pictures with the notes if one stared into the fire long enough. It told stories of adventure and freedom and companionship. Pat clapped her hands, and joined in singing:

A young native woman sitting next to Pat leaned forward, holding up a small beaded drum.

"Do you think they'll mind if I join in?"

"Make it so," Deb responded, already enthralled by the sounds. Deb nodded her head as the drummer joined in, hesitatingly at first, and then more strongly, instinctively filling in the empty spaces. She was like a weaver adding layers to a tapestry.

Willow and then Skylar stood up and started to slowly dance. They moved without any signs of self-consciousness: a small arm up here, a head turned there, step by step, they moved in place. Gracie joined them, her face like a little sun. Girl by little girl joined in, drawn by the magic of the music, dropping their shoes off and flinging their arms into the air.

"Come on, Grandma," Willow said, slightly impatient. "What are you waiting for? Wake up!" She stood with her hands on her small hips.

What am I waiting for indeed? Pat thought. Getting up from the log, she took the two small hands offered. Looking over at Deb, she saw Gracie pulling her own grandmother up to dance. They danced the music of the stars, the fire, and the waves on the beach. They danced all these things and more, joining with dancing females of all ages and sizes on the crowded beach. It was as if they were one body dancing in the dark.

This must be what it's like to fly, Pat thought. Time stretched and slowed to the sounds so that she couldn't even say how long they danced. Still, they danced on. She saw a gentle woman, coming around the lighted circle from the fire. She was illuminated by the glow as she bent to Pat's daughter, Sarah, and offered her a hand.

It's a magic night, Pat breathed with all her will. *It's a night to dance. Please, please, please accept her offer.* As if she heard her mother, Sarah looked across the flames and met her gaze. She sheepishly took the offered hand and started to dance. A night of new beginnings, Pat thought joyfully, her heart bursting and tears welling up in her eyes.

"Dance, Grandma, dance!" Skylar shouted, and they danced some more. Looking up at the full moon, Pat saw a crow, its beautiful blue-black feathers shining against the brightness of the full moon. She heard its cawing as it circled the fire, seeming to dance with them.

Leaving Gracie to dance, Deb sat down next to her mother, exhilarated by the dancing and the wonders before her eyes. The smoky smell of burned birch bark filled her spirit with peace. She breathed it in, remembering moments at camp as a child when all seemed well in the world.

Looking at the others gathered around the fire, she saw dancing fingers of flame reflected in their eyes. Across the fire, she noticed a young radiant woman nursing a newborn in a folding chair. Next to her sat a proud, attentive grandmother.

That's our new baby, Deb thought. *Born at solstice.*

"What's her name?" she asked.

"Summer Joy," the new mother replied.

Deb got up to take a closer look.

"Oh, what a beautiful baby," she said, touching the baby's cheek gently.

Two long-haired teenage girls sat gossiping quietly on large rocks, twirling their flip-flops around their toes, cell phones momentarily tucked away.

In the background, the drummer's beat was steady. A native woman stood. She had such presence everyone stilled naturally to listen. In a sing-song voice she began to speak.

"Madeline Island, the medicine island, gets its name because a native woman, a chief's daughter, fell in love with a white man. When they married, the dark robe gave her a name from the white man's religion, Madeline. But some say she had many names before that. Mida was one of them."

The woman's body began to sway to the drum.

"In the days when the island had almost as many trees as the fish surrounding it, a certain summer was late in coming. The People had kept warm and safe by helping each other through the long cold winter, but the spring refused to come, and they longed for the trees to leaf out and the sand to be warm between their toes. Even the trilliums, the most brave of flowers did not show their faces. Each day passed and still the sun refused to shine but a short time. Everyone – the birds, the deer, the little children – watched for the change. When none came, the People became afraid. *What could be keeping summer?*

"Finally, one morning, the chief took his daughter and called all the people together. 'Take the children,' he instructed Mida, 'to the other side of the island, and ask the ancestors for help, because if summer doesn't come soon, we will all starve.'

"The woman paused for a moment, looking to the west.

"It was cold, and some of the children complained or cried, but Mida made them continue. Finally reaching their destination, she built a big fire and as the smoke went up into the sky she sang their story, asking for help, and showing the children who would suffer if summer did not come. She pledged a bonfire and songs every solstice. Feeding the children the last of the wild rice bread, she led them back home again.

"Imagine their joy the next morning when a warm western wind blew over the island. The sun shone the longest that day that anyone could remember, and the birds sang their love songs and made nests. The trees blossomed out to hold those nests, and the deer found green grass to eat and were content.

"Filled with happiness, the People gathered together picking berries. The children ran until they lay tired by the shore, with enough fish caught to fill each and every belly. The chief suddenly realized his daughter was not there.

"'Where is Mida?' he cried out.

"'I am here,' a voice floated from the edge of the wood. Everyone turned and saw her approaching them, wild violets and trilliums wreathed in her hair. She joined them in their celebration. To this day, each year at solstice, keeping her promise, we build the fire and send up songs, and we believe she comes and brings the life of summer to her island."

The woman sat down amid applause and smiles.

As the music waned, a few women rejoined the fire circle, while others walked to get hot chocolate at a nearby table. Deb looked through the crowd of relaxed faces and caught Pat's eye. Seated to her right, Skylar sat on Pat's lap. Willow was asleep at her feet. All three of them looked positively blissful.

"Grammy, I want to dance some more!" Gracie called as she stood before Deb. Deb kissed her on the forehead.

"Come sit with me for awhile," she said, holding out her hands invitingly. "We'll dance in our minds."

"What does it matter?" Deb whispered to Pat. "In the end, this moment is all that is important."

"It doesn't matter if the retreat was chaotic," Pat agreed, nodding her head as if telepathically connected to Deb. "It doesn't even matter if a strange woman chooses to leave any way she wants."

"This was a great choice," Deb said, nodding to the circle. "I wouldn't have done it any other way.

"Look what happened," Pat replied, wrapping her sweatshirt tightly around Skylar against the night chill.

"We did it, girlfriend," Deb whispered to Pat.

"Amen to that."

Unnoticed by the happy crowd, as if on air, a woman with flowing hair continued to dance in the shadows.

In the cabin following the bonfire, Linda stood with a vacuum cleaner handle in her hand and looked around for an outlet. Music was playing from down the street. The room had an air of joyful lightheartedness. Deb, Pat and the other women were dancing and celebrating.

"Look at this mess!" Linda said in frustration.

The women stopped dancing and stared in silence at Linda for a moment. No one moved. No one seemed to know how to respond. Julie and Noreen look embarrassed. No one wanted to challenge her.

"I think I'm ready for bed after such a long day. I'd like to go back next door," Julie suggested.

"I'll go with you," Noreen agreed.

"I want to walk down to the dock to look for the northern lights," Deb suggested. "Anyone want to come?"

"I'm in!" Pat answered.

"Who's going to watch out for the wild creatures of the night?" Carolyn wondered.

"Aw, come on you crazy women, let's all go. There's safety in numbers," Julie said.

Bev walked with her walker over to Linda in silence and gave her a hug. Linda stood alone in the middle of the room, holding the handle of the vacuum.

Carolyn came back in the door and deliberately walked over to the pile of journals. She picked up the journal with the entry that Linda had read earlier and pointed to a passage.

Isn't there more to life than duty or responsibility?

"Weren't you the one who told us about this?" she asked compassionately. She turned around and left to rejoin the others at the dock, leaving Linda alone with her thoughts.

Linda stood stock-still.

Why aren't I that woman?

She threw down the vacuum, grabbed her jacket, and followed the laughing voices of the others into the darkness. The dog followed her out the door.

I may not be that woman, but I can be free. I know what I'm choosing, she thought.

The empty cabin was left with lights on, door open, and vacuum in the middle of the floor.

The women lay on the dock under the star-filled sky. Overhead, the light from the full moon enveloped them in energizing and silky iridescence.

"Ah whooo...," Deb called loudly toward the lake, cupping her hands around her mouth.

"Sounds like a dying loon," Julie teased. "Let me try." She held her hands in front of her face as if in prayer and let loose with a near perfect loon call. A call came back from across the lake.

"Look! There's the North Star!" Linda said.

"Where?" Deb asked. "Glad you made it, girlfriend," she added, noticing Linda's presence.

"Over there at the end of the handle for the Big Dipper," she instructed. Deb looked up and noticed the telltale streaks of light in the northern sky.

Can it really be? Yes!

"Do you see what I see?" Deb asked, pointing upward.

"Is that northern lights?" Carolyn wondered.

"Yup. Aurora Borealis... now there's a rare sight."

The women stayed for a long time watching the kaleidoscopic green, white, and pink swirls of cosmic energy in the sky above them.

"It's like watching the creation of the universe all over again," Deb said with awe in her voice.

Linda felt a buzz in her pocket. Pulling out her phone, she noticed her husband's picture smiling at her from the screen. Inhaling deeply of the night air, she smiled serenely and went off to answer the call.

A sudden movement drew Deb's gaze towards the bushes down the beach. Squinting, she barely made out the dark shadow of a human form lurking off to the side, as if it was watching the women.

"Time to go back," Deb said, suddenly feeling the night air on her neck.

There couldn't really be someone watching us, could there?

"Is someone there?" she called out. "Why don't you come and join us?"

The only response to her entreaty was the sound of waves lapping the shore.

The other women continued watching the night sky.

I'm not going to let some shadow wreck this whole evening, Deb thought.

"Want me to walk back with you?" Deb offered, noticing Bev's yawn. "Long day, huh?"

"But great," Bev replied.

Soon, they were back in the cabin, Deb lying on the couch in front of a crackling fire in the wood stove. Her mind was ruminating on details.

"Everything has been going great. I just wish we knew what happened to that woman!" Deb exclaimed into the air above her. "It's like a story with the last three pages missing. I just can't leave it alone. I can't stand the thought that someone may have been pushed off the ferry... or worse yet, jumped! If she jumped, what would cause someone to do such a thing?"

Bev listened quietly to Deb, waiting for her to finish.

"It's just so hard for me to imagine someone doing that," Deb finished.

A long pause fell between the two women as they looked at each other in the firelight.

"Do you remember that talk we had on the ferry?" Bev asked softly. "We were talking about some reasons why someone's life could be bad enough for them to want to end it all."

"Sure, I remember. I was there."

"I believe we all have those 'I never thought this would happen to me' moments in our lives," Bev said. "We can each fill in the blanks on that one. For me, it was the day I received my diagnosis."

"I understand." Deb nodded. "Heaven knows I have had my own share of heavy heartbreak. For me, life always seemed to snatch me back from the jaws of darkness and light a pathway out."

"I remember the day that my doctor told me," Bev said softly. "It felt like a death sentence. In the end, it was the beginning of the end of a long struggle over my own stubbornness, a journey towards accepting the new order."

"I know what you mean."

"We all have to decide whether we're going to jump or not," Bev chided. "We all get to choose how we see and interact with the world... as for the woman on the ferry, we may never know the last chapter. It's her book."

With that, Bev set down her cup of tea, leaned back in her chair and closed her eyes. There would be no bad dreams chasing after her. She had defeated her demons long ago.

Deb could hear the other women giggling their way up the path.

"I'm going to bed," Deb said. "It's time for me to go next door. Have a good night."

"Sweet dreams," Bev replied.

Deb picked up the latest Kate Mosse novel, returning to her marked page and reaching for a dark chocolate bar on the bedside table. The hour was late, and she could no longer hear the voices of women walking down the street or the splash of bodies as they made one last plunge into the cold water. The wind had died down as if sleeping for the night, and the cabin was blessedly quiet.

Old habits are hard to break, she thought as she took another nibble. This one is never going to be broken.

By any measure, she should have been cozy. The comforter was light and airy, and she had two big poofy pillows to lean on. Everyone was safely back in their cabin. She had talked to Marc and learned that all was well at home. The book was fun and engaging. But somehow she couldn't lose herself in it like she normally did.

Realizing she had gone a couple of pages without really reading, Deb broke off one more piece of chocolate and slowly let it melt in her mouth. She found herself thinking about the man in the woods.

Who was he, really? She shuddered. The thought of him nibbled on the edge of her consciousness like a little mouse. *Of course he wasn't really evil. He was just a man. Probably that guy the bartender was talking about.* Her eyes widened at the thought. *Sure he was... the land developer. But there was something more about him. He seemed like bad news, and the way the bartender talked, he could have really hurt someone.*

Had he taken the woman out in those same woods? Right where they met him? Had he dragged her past the bushes, into the dense pines, and... No, she stopped herself. *Bev was right. It might not be my story. I'm not going to think about it tonight.* Consciously changing her thoughts she started to say her nightly prayers to the universe. Halfway through, her eyelids got heavy.

Where am I? I'm back in the woods. But how can this be? Deb looked around squinting in the gathering dusk, trying to get her bearings. Glancing around, she saw Pat walking beside her. "Where are we going?' she asked, but Pat didn't reply. A bat swooped down from the branches above and she automatically ducked, covering her hair.

Silly, she thought, *bats don't really get caught in your hair.*

The stifling fog was back and enveloped her, penetrating deep within her, like a cold rainy day on the big lake. *I'll never be warm again.* Her breath constricted, like there was an anvil on her chest. The fog left a narrow path to walk through but tugged at her nightgown as if it were alive.

What's happening? she thought. *This is wrong. We didn't come back out here, I'm in my bed.* "Pat," she tried calling out, but her voice failed her. She could hear noises of Ferris wheels and barkers ahead, and as they moved forward they became louder and louder.

"Why, it's a carnie!" Deb exclaimed, the lights so bright she could hardly keep her eyes open.

Standing in the center of a chaotic clearing was the land developer, juggling.

"Step right up, ladies! Buy a condo and win a prize."

"Stop that right now!" Deb said. "You can't sell off Madeline Island."

But he only kept juggling.

"Run, run, run, as fast as you can, you can't stop me, I'm the flimflam man. You, too, can be a winner." Reaching out as if to grab her as Deb rushed by, his laughter echoed behind them.

Turning a corner, she ran into a young woman in a waitress uniform running in the opposite direction.

"Sorry, sorry," she panted as she pushed by. "But I've got to get to the ferry before he catches up."

Debs eyes followed her as she was swallowed up in the dark, a man chasing close behind.

"Don't let him catch you," she called out.

Stopping to look around, she spotted a circlet of light off to the side.

"Maybe we should check it out," she said to Pat, and without waiting, she stepped off the path into the fog. Before her was a huge bed, covered in money. Sitting square in the center was a familiar figure, the rich man who lived on the island. On one side of him was his lover, and the other, his wife.

This just gets weirder and weirder, she thought, stepping closer. The wife was showering him with dollar bills, while the other woman was busy stuffing them into a pillowcase. The wife had a hard smile on her face, and Deb saw that she held a pillow behind her back and was slowly pulling it out, moving it closer and closer to his face. Pat pulled on Deb's arm, taking her back to the path.

They were suddenly alerted by the sound of sobbing.

"What's that?"

Moving slowly, they came upon a woman on a chair, face in her hands. Pat moved to comfort her, but stopped when the woman lifted her face

"You can't get in here," she called out, "and I can't get out, don't you see? The cell bars are all around me. Do you have a key?" she asked hopefully. As far as Deb could tell, there were no visible bars, just a stool on which she sat.

Shaking her head and wishing that she had a key, she watched as Lotta started to cry again. Turning, she reached out to Pat. Before she could even call her name, she felt herself falling, down... down... down.

Will I ever stop falling? She anticipated the hard ground coming to meet her body, wishing she still had a few extra pounds of fat to shield the impact. *What a silly thought!* Somehow it made her feel a bit better. *I'm falling endlessly through space.*

Just as she reached the ground and braced her body for the blow, she felt hands on the back of her neck, gripping it tightly.

Help me! she screamed. *I need help!*

"You don't need my help," a calming voice replied. "You know you're strong. There is evil in the world, it's true. But you are only dreaming. Come, take my hand. I'll bring you back. But I can't stay. I have much to do tonight."

Deb felt a hand on hers. And it was enough.

She jolted upright, her whole body perspiring, and rubbed her eyes. *It was only a dream. I dropped off while reading or saying my prayers, and I dreamt it all.*

She took a deep cleansing breath, willing her heart to slow down to a normal beat. Quietly, so she wouldn't wake the others, she went into the bathroom and washed her face and hands. Then she cupped her hands and drank some of the cold water. It tasted so good.

A dream, she thought, going back to bed and turning out the light. *Only a dream. But was it? It sure felt real. Who was that who helped me? And where was Pat when I needed her?*

Determined to get back to sleep and trying to convince herself, she lay down.

Only a dream, she thought, repeating it like a mantra in her mind. *Only a dream. But still, wait till I tell Pat about this one. No. I'm not going to wait until the sun comes up, when I feel too silly to tell her.* Pulling down the covers and putting her feet firmly on the floor, she padded her way into the next room to tell Pat.

Pat was still awake.

Deb's hesitantly pushed open the door. Pat pulled back the covers and moved over to make room, open to hearing whatever she had to say.

Chapter Twenty-Two
June 23

"Pat, what in heaven's name is the matter?" asked Deb, opening her friend's bedroom door the next morning. "You look worried." *You look distracted*, she thought. *Two eggs short of a dozen.*

"I'm okay." Pat got up from the bed, her words meant to assure herself more than Deb. Walking past the antique dresser mirror, she saw a strange woman looking back at her, hair like a peacock's feathers sticking out and up in the back of her head. Pushing it down, it immediately popped right back up.

"I was thinking about the woman, you know, Mida, the one that disappeared.

"You gave her a name?"

"Just so I could think more clearly about her. I know it's not her real name." She was busy pulling things out of her overnight bag.

"Aha, she said triumphantly, pulling out a hair brush and trying to get her hair under control. "I think I know where she is."

"Really?" Deb asked skeptically, sitting down on the bed to listen. "Did it come to you in a hot flash dream? One of those personal hot tropical moments?"

"I would rather not talk about menopause, if you please," Pat said, concentrating on her brushing.

"Enough," Deb said impatiently. "Talk."

"Well, I still think she's not a real woman at all."

"How did you come to that conclusion? You mean she's a man dressed as a woman?"

"No, that would be interesting, but too silly."

As if any idea was too silly for you, Deb thought.

"No, it's a lot of stuff that has been happening: the journals and what some of the other women have said." Putting down the brush, Pat turned to face Deb.

"And I swear I saw her take Sarah's hand at the fire last night. Really. And what about the dream you shared with me last night?"

"That was just a person and my dream wasn't real," Deb said, trying hard to forget how she had felt in the dark the night before.

"Dreams are sometimes more real than you think."

"I know, but who else saw her at the fire?"

"Lots of folks. But listen, please. I went around asking, and the strangest part is she always looked different to each person. Sarah, for instance, saw the woman as a grandmotherly type, and I saw her as my age."

"Ahuh," Deb said. "Like you're not a grandmotherly type? Sorry, it just doesn't make sense to me. Why would she use the ferry to escape?"

"Okay, this is the crazy part. I think she belongs to the island. She could be some spirit that protects it and the people here, and at solstice she leaves it for a day or so and then comes back to start the new cycle all over again."

"Puh lease. What has that Doc been giving you for menopause? Ask her if I can have some. Do you think she's some kind of Zen Goddess of the island or something?"

"Maybe. Remember what that woman said to you on the bench the other day? Come on Deb, listen to me. This is important." She turned away sighing.

Deb took the brush from her and began to brush Pat's hair.

"I'm just trying to understand."

"Anyway, whether it's a spirit or not, I don't think they'll ever find her. She just isn't meant to be found."

Maybe, just maybe, Deb thought, shaking her head, skeptically.

"Yeah sure," she said. "Tell me, friend, just how are you going to spin that one for our dear detective?

"Easy," Pat said with a grin. "I'll just convince his wife, and she'll convince him!"

"I'll be right back," Pat said to the others. They were picking up trash on the street outside Lotta's and putting it into the can tied to the back of Bev's scooter. "I have to clean off the message board." Pat walked up to the board posted outside the door. There were several scraps of paper tacked to it. She reached up and took them down in turn. Reading each one, she smiled.

> Noreen: Remember to call your mother.
> She's waiting to hear from you.

> Thanks for the great time! See you next year.

> Next year, ask Coco's to cater the food. (Just kidding)

She reached for the last note, written in perfect small script.

> Pat and Deb: Happy summer solstice. Thanks for coming.
> I was trying to think of a gift I could give you two, so I decided
> to give you a mystery. Hope you enjoyed it. Safe travels.

Pat re-read the last note and shook her head. Folding it in half, she tucked it carefully into her pocket and walked towards the cabin.

"Thanks for the gift," she said, raising her face to the sky and laughing out loud. Thinking of the good coffee awaiting her, she left to meet her friends and help finish the cleanup.

"Need more coffee?"

"You bet." Pat held up her cup. "This has definitely been an espresso weekend."

"I know what you mean," the Beach Club waitress said. She hesitated. "Can I sit down for a moment?"

"Sure," Pat said, looking up in surprise and pulling out a chair. "What's up?"

"Sorry to interrupt, but I heard you might be looking for me." She noticed Pat's blank stare. "I think I'm one of your missing women. At least, that's what your mother told me."

The woman now had Pat's full attention.

"Tiny old wrinkled woman with a fancy cane?"

"And great clothes? Yes, that's her."

"So Mom thought you might be the missing woman? For a dead woman, you look pretty lively to me."

The girl chuckled nervously.

"Your Mom was in this morning. Jessie, right? And she got to talking..."

"That's my Mom alright."

"So, she told me who your missing suspects were, and she thought I was the missing girlfriend." The woman looked around to see if anyone needed coffee.

"Just a minute," she said, getting up and making a quick round with the pot. She returned to the table and settled back in. "You see, I had a fight with my boyfriend, and well, more than a fight, and I went over on the ferry for the day to clear my head. The very same ferry when someone was thought to disappear. So, is it me?"

The woman acted like she was in some Agatha Christie mystery, and was about to win the prize.

"Tell me one thing," Pat said. "Did you leave a note?"

"A note? No," she said, with a puzzled expression. "I don't think... wait a minute, I started to leave one for my roommate, and then I lost it. Is that the one you mean?"

"That might be it. Thanks, and congratulations."

"For what?"

"For being alive."

"You're welcome. Gotta go."

As she rose to leave, Pat stopped her.

"Just one more question, if you don't mind. I'm curious. Why did you come back?"

The woman thought for a minute.

"I wasn't going to. The strangest thing happened. While I was sitting over at the Big Water Café in Bayfield waiting for my ride, a woman came over with the pot and offered me another cup of coffee. I remember feeling grateful because I always pour coffee for other people.

"'Looks like you've been having a hard time,' the woman said.

"I burst into tears. After I told her what had happened, she said an interesting thing. She said – and I'll never forget it – you don't have to give up something you love because you're afraid. And I decided she was right. Then the woman got up and moved away.

"Oh, and here's your mother's tab. She said you were good for it." As the waitress stood, her thoughts had already returned to the extra tips she had made during the retreat.

Can't wait to get to Duluth for the Macy's sale, she thought.

Mothers, Pat thought.

Chapter Twenty-Three
June 23

Noticing that Bev hadn't come inside with the others, Pat walked up behind Bev on the street as she was packing up her Tarot paraphernalia.

"Need help?"

Bev hesitated only a moment.

"Yes, that would be great. Can you help me with this table?"

"Sure." Pat started to collapse the card table. "I've been thinking about that reading you did for me the other day."

Bev's cheeks pinked.

"It was pretty terrible. Sorry. I'm really just learning, and sometimes I say stuff that makes me just want to poke out my third eye."

Pat laughed.

"Funny! No, really, I think the cards were spot on. I was that silly Jester in the middle of things making a whirlwind with this retreat. Trouble is, the cards were true. We just weren't interpreting them quite right."

"Isn't that the way it goes?" Bev pulled out a notebook from her pile of books. "Lets see, here it is. Five of Pentacles reversed could mean there will be strife, but it doesn't have to have a bad outcome. So that would be the retreat, I guess. For this card, it's all in the attitude. And you are the Jester," she said, looking up and softening the words with a smile. "At least in this reading."

"The Chariot card represents you at your worst, when you always feel you know best no matter what, or, at your best, you helping and making things better. Then there were the Tower and Swords cards. You could think of the missing woman being away in the tower, but that could mean either it's because she was being held, as shown by the presence of the swords, or because of her choosing to take herself away. Maybe your theory of the woman being a spirit could fit for her."

"The Devil card could be about a battle of light and dark at solstice, and evil appearing to get the upper hand," Pat said.

"But in the end, the Death card could mean new beginnings, for you, or for the island, rather than the actual death of the woman."

They looked at each other.

"So, do you want me to do another reading?" Bev asked, with a twinkle in her eye, "not the third one. I've got my cards right here," she said, holding up her hand.

Pat hugged her.

"Actually, I would, but not now. In the end, I guess I know it's always up to me what happens."

"Spoken like a true Jester. Pat, there's something else I want to tell you."

"What?"

"I knew about Lotta, but I didn't tell anyone."

"Why not?"

"She's my friend. And once you say something, there's no taking it back. Maybe you should talk to her."

Pat nodded.

They packed everything up and headed inside to meet their friends.

Deb sat out on the front steps of the cabin, enjoying the moment of waiting for the others to finish packing.

As she looked around, she noticed that the foliage on the trees seemed to be bursting with crisp greens. The grass was still kissed with dew. Lupine and trillium were in full bloom in the beds around the steps.

Deb inhaled, feeling gratitude and taking in a breath of fresh, crisp air. A line of women meandered happily past her, pulling suitcases behind them as they made their way to the ferry.

A young girl ran up to Deb, thrusting a small bouquet of Johnny jump-ups into her hands.

"Here," she said with a shy smile. "Thanks for inviting us." She turned and ran quickly to her place in line. Deb waved her hand at the mother who was patting the child on the back.

"Thanks," the woman mouthed back.

Chapter Twenty-Four
June 23

Walking inside the cabin, Deb and Pat sat with their friends, enjoying one last chat before leaving. Their packed bags were piled next to the doorway.

"So you didn't have to convince anyone about your weird theory? And that's it?'

"Yup, I think so." Pat leaned back on her chair legs just like she always told her son not to. She ran her fingers through bangs that flopped right back down on her forehead.

"Let's see, Gary says…"

"Wait a sec," Noreen interrupted. "The detective lets you call him Gary now?"

"Sure. At least when he's not around to hear it," Pat said a little sheepishly.

Everyone laughed.

"Anyway, do you want to know the scoop, or not?"

"Oh, oh, someone didn't get her nap," Julie teased.

Pat pretended to scowl.

"Come on, Pat, we're dying to hear," Bev said. "We've been so busy 'retreating,' by which I mean leading workshops, serving meals, and picking up garbage, that we haven't had a lot of time to figure out the mystery."

"Yeah, remind me to be gone when these two invite us again for a relaxing weekend retreat," Carolyn agreed.

"Oh, come on, Carolyn. You know you had a great time."

"I did," she admitted. "But fill us in. What happened to our suspects, and was there really a woman?"

"Let's see," Pat said. "LeSeur found the woman that Deb heard about from the jealous wife. Remember the one who was cheating with her husband? My goodness, I almost pity that poor husband. I said I *almost* pity him," she added, after noticing their surprised stares. "It turns out the woman went off to her mother's home to reconsider her role of being the other woman. She decided she just wasn't cut out for it."

"Especially," Pat said with a twinkle, "when she found out that her boy-friend's wife was the one with all the money and not him."

"I never thought that one was a real candidate, but what about my guy in the bathroom?" Carolyn asked eagerly. "Now, there's a real suspect. He had motive and opportunity. And he was horrible. You didn't hear him. I did."

"I'm surprised you could hear him through the wall. What did you do, put your ear up against it?" Linda teased. "I'll bet the F.B.I. would just love to sign you up for bathroom duty."

"Well, you're right," Pat interrupted, "he did have opportunity, and he is certainly a bad character, but it turns out he was just showing off to his friend. I just talked to his girlfriend at the Beach Club, where she works as a waitress. He hit her once and she was gone. Unfortunately for him she has two big brothers. You won't be listening to him through bathroom walls anytime soon."

"So that leaves the creepy guy we met in the woods," Deb said. "We think he was the land developer that we heard about from the bartender."

"You mean the land raper?" Julie asked.

"Whatever... his girlfriend... she did leave on that ferry, or one pretty close to it. But here's the part that's right out of a novel. She was headed for the B.I.A., the Bureau of Indian Affairs, in Ashland. While the local authorities were looking for her, she was meeting with federal agents."

"It's not illegal to buy land from Natives, is it?" Bev asked.

"No, it's not," Deb said. "But it is illegal to set up an elaborate scam, which he had done before in Arizona and Oklahoma. Naturally, they didn't get him on that. Can you guess what they got him on?"

Everyone was silent, waiting for the answer.

"I know, I know," Carolyn said. "Taxes. It's the way they always get the mob guys."

"And the prize goes to Carolyn," Pat said. "That guy's gonna get ten to twenty, since they have a great witness who is willing to testify."

"Don't forget Lotta," Julie said.

"Lotta's our friend. She's done everything with us," Noreen said. "We don't even know why she was in prison."

"I know," Bev confessed. "It was self-defense. He was drunk and coming at her."

"I've seen lots of cases like that," Deb said. "A woman makes a split second decision that changes her whole life."

"Enough with suspects. Did a body ever turn up?" Linda asked.

"Nope. The Coast Guard searched a long time. On the other hand, the water is cold and deep. But, I still say there never was a real woman at all," Pat said stubbornly. "Maybe, she was something else."

"Stop, Pat, with the woo-woo theories," Julie admonished. "All I can say is, if you think so, then at least... Hell no, you're not my guru, and since you're not wearing your collar, I'm not required to believe you. But, let's raise a glass to her, whoever she was, and to next year's retreat as well."

And glasses were raised by all.

"Before you leave," Deb said, standing up and walking to the kitchen. "I have something for each of you."

"What's this?"

Returning to the room, she opened a shopping bag and pulled out a matching sweatshirt for each of them. Embroidered on the front were the words: "First Annual M.I. Solstice Retreat."

"Just a little something from Pat and me to express our gratitude. Thanks for helping us. We couldn't have done it without you."

After the others had gone outside to load the cars, Deb sat pensively at the kitchen table, pen in hand, staring at the journal before her. She began to write.

June 23

I came here three days ago to gather with close friends and family. Little did I know that my dream of a simple, relaxing retreat would evolve into a major happening. Hundreds of women joined us unexpectedly. Despite my worst fears, all have lived to tell another tale. I must remember that things are never as bad as they seem.

I encountered a mystery woman this week through these journals, where her presence shone through like a light. Sometimes, I believe that I caught real glimpses of her. Other times, I wonder if I have gone over the edge.

Is she the Spirit of Madeline Island? Or some kind of guardian angel who ministers to troubled seekers who arrive here? Is sh a figment of my imagination made real by the potent magic that exists in the natural beauty of this place? Did I conjure an imaginary spirit out of my need to cope with dark forces? Or, more likely, was I awake long enough to catch a glimpse of the light that is ever present in the world, but especially visible here? Maybe she comes now and Zen.

I haven't yet decided. I hope to learn more in future visits. We have already reserved this cabin for next year's summer solstice. I can't wait to find out if my new friend pays a visit then.

For now, we say goodbye to this place of respite. Armed with renewed hope, it's off to the daily grind.

Thank you, Madeline, for helping us and teaching us that light will always be stronger than darkness because of the power called Love.

Gratefully,
Deb

After carefully placing the notebook on the counter, Deb looked around and turned off the lights, putting the key in the lock on the way out.

Standing on the ferry's upper deck, Pat gazed toward the dock of La Pointe as it became smaller and smaller in her vision.

It looks like the scene from that play, Brigadoon, she thought, *fading away into the fog.*

"It looks like a fairy tale place, doesn't it?" Deb put her arm around her friend, once again reading her mind. "And that woman... I really believe we met her coming off the ferry that first day; you know the one who helped me when my shoe was once again untied. She just touched me for a second, you know? But she was like Mother Earth and the Wizard of Oz all rolled into one. I guess even if I never find out who she was for sure, I'm glad she's a part of the island. Can you believe it?"

That's my trouble, Pat thought, *believing.*

Squinting, she could just make out a figure in a long flowing dress, standing on the edge of the dock, waving cheerily, as if right at her.

Is it the pastor? she thought, waving back. *No, no. I know she's back at the church. Could it possibly be her? After a whole weekend of trying to find her?* There waving on the dock? Pointing wordlessly, she directed Deb's gaze to the shore.

"Oh, my gosh!" Deb smiled and clapped her hands joyfully. "It's her! I know it is. She came to see us off."

Pat was more skeptical, but then she took a deep breath. There are moments in life when one is called to leap. Church people might call it a leap of faith. Others might call it a leap into the unknown.

In the end, Pat thought, *it's choosing. It's whistling in the dark; reaching out a hand when you don't know it will be taken; or believing enough to act.*

I've had trouble with leaping. That's why I am so proud of my friends. I recognize courageous acts when I see them... Maybe that's what a pastor is... a cheerleader urging others on from the sidelines, like Moses, never reaching the Promised Land myself. Heavens, I've been reading the Bible too long.

"I believe it's her," she said out loud, leaping, for once. "And that's enough." Feeling for one precious moment that everything was in balance and that somehow it was because of Mida, she watched, straining her eyes as the fog closed in and the image on the dock seemed to break apart into a million pieces of light.

Waving once more, she turned to Mike who had come out on the deck to stand by her. "Some weekend, huh?" he asked, rubbing his neck with his big hand.

Pat shook her head and drew in a breath of the cool clear air.

"You can say that again, big guy. You need me to rub that spot?" Reaching up, she skillfully pressed her fingers into the tender spots. "Wow, you are tight. You know you did the best anyone could, don't you?"

"Right," he said, stretching. "It's just that I always prided myself in the numbers. Can you believe it? How many trips back and forth? How many people? Crap! Excuse me, how much money we took in!" He turned to look at Pat, and she dropped her hands. "But now, because of this one weekend, I won't ever look at being captain in the same way again." Looking off to the horizon, he continued softly speaking. "These are real souls I'm here to protect and care for as they travel these waters. They always were, but now I know it to my core. It's changed everything for me. He was silent then, having said more words than she had ever heard him string together before. He was a man of few words. Between friends, words are seldom needed.

Epilogue
July 24

A single gull soared back and forth on the lake's wind currents under the fluffy clouds of another azure Lake Superior sky.

"Glad you could make it, Berni," Deb said softly, looking up from the deck of the Hotel Chequamegon, remembering her first born who had already crossed over. "Wish I could fly with you today." Hearing footsteps, she looked across the deck to see a familiar form walking towards her.

Pat sat down in the chair next to the table with a satisfied sigh.

"Hi, kiddo. Did you order yet? Sorry I'm late. Even though it's been a month since the retreat, I'm still answering emails."

"Don't worry, be happy," Deb said. "Nope, I didn't order, I just had coffee." Pat reached down and patted Strider, scratching him in the places only a true friend could know about. Strider had been dancing by his owner's chair but now settled in on Deb's feet with a blissful expression.

"Glad to see you too, old man." Pat couldn't help smiling back at the only smiling dog she had ever known.

"I think everything is finally done," Pat continued, turning back to Deb. "Last thank-you sent, last vendor paid, and we have ended up with a whopping one hundred twenty-six dollars and fifty-one cents."

"Great. So, we actually paid our expenses?"

"Not exactly. But we got a great deal on the cabin, and Lotta says our next breakfast is on her."

"So, you've talked to Lotta?"

"Yes, and I'm glad I did. She's doing okay. Turns out everyone on the island knew her secret, and they were protecting her."

"Oh, that's good, and the woman?"

"I talked to Gary just this morning. They're closing the case. The official verdict is just a miscount on the ferry. Mike is upset, of course, that they counted wrong, but he was relieved that his record as captain is untainted." After they ordered, they sat in companionable silence.

"So what do you think?" Pat asked.

"Think? Think about what?" Deb answered, her mind lost in the water and the sun.

"So what do you think we're going to do for our winter solstice retreat?" Deb laughed.

"Give me a break, or at least another cup of coffee before we even think about doing it." Leaning down she took Strider's muzzle in her hand.

"What do you think, dog? Should we get on this merry-go-round again?" Strider woofed.

Pat's phone rang.

"It's Bev," she said to Deb, recognizing the number.

Pat held up the phone so they could both hear.

"I'm calling to thank you again for the wonderful weekend up there and to say goodbye before I leave," Bev said.

"Where are you going this time?" Pat asked. "Off on another adventure?"

"I'm off to Taos, New Mexico. I met a wonderful woman at the retreat from there, and I decided since I had so much positive feedback from my readings, I would try my sleight of hand in the big time. Wish me luck!"

"Luck. Just try not to give anyone a reading like mine, okay?"

"Right. Have you heard from Linda? I just can't get over the change in her. I saw she and her husband in church Sunday, and it's as if they were on a second honeymoon. But it's more than that. She seems so relaxed. She whispered to me during the announcements that she's giving up sitting on all those church boards. I'm telling you, neither of us can wait until next year's retreat."

Pat laughed at the thought.

"Well, I've got to go wash clothes so I can pack," Bev said. "And Pat?

Thanks again. See you, Deb!"

"It was our pleasure," Pat replied, as she hung up.

Hooray! Pat thought. She sent up a silent cheer to the universe.

"Look, I have another message on my phone," Pat said, pushing the button that leads to her voicemail. "It's my mother."

Beep. "Millie and I had so much fun, we've decided to take you up on your generous offer to go on a bridge cruise. I know, I know... she hasn't ever played bridge before, but we'll be fine. Maybe we'll meet some men. Wouldn't that be something? Call me." Beep.

PROLOGUE FOR UPCOMING BOOK:
Murder on the Bridge

IT STARTED OUT as a lark. Their daughters were the ones who had suggested a bridge cruise – a well-needed getaway, some time in the sun. It's the kind of thing older women do for a little safe fun: playing cards, and to be perfectly honest, finding a man or two who can still stay awake long enough to take a turn around the dance floor at night. "A Disney cruise for the elderly," Jessie had said. They had laughed.

But this was no ordinary cruise, because a bridge cruise usually means cards and fun, not a body taking a header off the captain's bridge in the middle of the night. Add to the mix that "the body" is the most eligible man on the boat. What starts out as a fun way to spend a week meeting new people, turns into a frightening nightmare, as Deb and Pat's mothers try to solve the murder before someone else gets pushed.

Chapter One

"What do you think? Will they actually go?" asked Deb, looking across at her friend, Pat, as they enjoyed a cup of coffee together.

"You got me. After all, she's your mother."

"And yours. Don't forget Jessie. What were you thinking of when you brought up a bridge cruise to them?"

Deb looked over accusingly.

"Frankly, I never thought they would take me up on it. A cruise in the West Indies? Come on. I just thought I would be a good daughter and offer it, and they would refuse. End of story. It was your idea to offer to pay for the trip. Jeeze Louise, like my mother would ever turn down a free trip."

"Well it was your idea to take them clothes shopping. My feet still hurt." Deb groaned. "Who would have thought two ladies in their eighties and nineties would be able to shop that long. I figured they would buy one full-bodied swim suit and sturdy tennis shoes. No, your mother had to have a designer dress. And five shops later they were giggling like school girls."

"Okay, okay. But at least the hard part is over. All we really have to do is pick them up and get them to the airport on time. And maybe after dropping them off, we can stop at the casino, win a little money, and have dinner." Pat smiled, thinking of two carefree weeks.

"You're right. And the up side is two carefree weeks, where we know they won't be getting into trouble," she said, as if reading Deb's mind.

Sitting in the afternoon sun, the two friends, both, after all, their mothers' daughters, had no idea what was coming next.

Recipes for Retreats

MITCH'S MOLE (MO-LAY) SAUCE

Mitch loves to cook. It's a love gift he gives to his wife like some men give pearls. His mole sauce is really great, but don't be afraid to experiment with your own. Just don't forget to add his secret ingredient: love.

INGREDIENTS

- 4 1/2 cups chicken broth
- 3 tablespoons olive oil
- 1 cup finely chopped onions
- 3 tablespoons chopped garlic
- 1 teaspoon dried oregano
- 1 teaspoon ground cumin
- 1/4 teaspoon ground cinnamon
- 2 1/2 tablespoons chili powder
- 3 tablespoons all-purpose flour
- 2 ounces dark chocolate, chopped
- 2 1/2-3 lb. chicken (fryer) brown and set aside

DIRECTIONS

Heat oil in a large saucepan over medium low heat. Add onion, garlic, oregano, cumin and cinnamon. Cover and cook until onion is almost tender, stirring occasionally – about 10 minutes. Mix in chili powder and flour; stir for 3 minutes.

Gradually whisk in chicken broth.

Increase heat to medium high.

Boil until reduced, about 35 minutes, stirring occasionally.

Remove from heat. Whisk in chocolate; season with salt and pepper, if desired. Add chicken to sauce and cover and simmer 30 minutes on low heat.

Serve over cooked noodles or rice.

JESSIE'S VENISON DISH

Venison, (that's deer, for city folks) is a wonderful meat, but it can be quite gamey. Excuse the pun. It's a good idea to make sure you take off the tallow (fat), especially if you put it in a stew or as with this recipe, with tomatoes. As a child, I grew up eating wild game and birds through the winter, and my mother, Jessie, became an expert at cooking it. I can still remember the scent of this stew as I came in the door from school.

INGREDIENTS

    1 1/2 lb. venison cut into strips.

    (You can use the chops if you have them.)

    2 cloves fresh garlic crushed.

    4 tablespoons butter (Venison is very lean.)

    2 large mild onions, sliced

    2 green peppers, cut in strips

    3 fresh tomatoes chunked (but canned works well too)

    1/4 cup of water

    1 cup of beef broth

    2 tablespoons cornstarch (my mother sometimes just used
       a can of mushroom soup – saves the gravy making)

    2 tablespoons soy sauce

    3 cups of cooked wild rice and 3/4 cup of white rice uncooked

DIRECTIONS

Brown garlic, onions and green pepper in butter till soft and then add meat, browning it. Add tomatoes and broth. Cover and simmer on low heat at least 30 minutes. Blend water, corn-starch and soy sauce. Stir into pan until thickened. Some people like to serve it over the rice, but I like to put the rice in the last 5 minutes so that it soaks up the flavor. Remember to cook the wild rice well; otherwise you'll have venison and hard rocks for supper. Soy sauce adds the needed saltiness, but flavor with salt and pepper to your taste.

SUNDAY BRUNCH EGG CASSEROLE

This lovely recipe is accredited to Sally Cole in the 1984 edition of the *Madeline Island Historical Cookbook*. I don't know if they are in print or not anymore. I got my copy from an elderly friend. Its fun to think this was indeed served out on the island, maybe even at St. John's Church.

INGREDIENTS

    2 cans cream of chicken soup
    1/2 cup white wine
    4 tablespoons minced onions
    2 cups shredded Swiss cheese
    1 teaspoon prepared brown mustard
    12 eggs
    1/2 whole milk
    12 thick French bread slices, buttered and halved

DIRECTIONS

Combine soup, milk, wine, onion and mustard. Cook, stirring until smooth and heated through. Stir in cheese until melted. Pour 1 cup of sauce into each of two 10 x 16 baking dishes. Break six eggs into sauce in each dish. Carefully spoon remaining sauce around eggs. Stand French bread around edges of casseroles with crusts up. Bake at 350 for 20 minutes or until set. Serves 12.

JFW (JUST FOR WOMEN) FROZEN SLUSH

Okay, so men can drink it, too, if there is some left over. Just think of this as what women drink when they want to get together and let their hair down.

INGREDIENTS

> 3 1/2 cup water
>
> 6 small cans frozen lemonade
>
> 1 cup sugar
>
> 1/2 quart vodka
>
> 2 tea bags, or 2 teaspoons instant tea
>
> 6 small cans frozen orange juice

DIRECTIONS

Stir water and sugar until dissolved, boiling a short time. (Not too much!) Put tea bags into the sugar water. Let stand until cool. Add orange juice, lemonade and vodka. Freeze overnight or longer. Stir every once in a while, if you think of it. Recipe freezes to a slush. To serve, pull out pretty glasses (I warned you it was for the girls), and put 1-2 tablespoons in glass, then fill with a sour mix.

Cheers, but be careful. After two glasses, secrets start to be shared whether you want them to be, or not!

CUP OF WITCHES' BREW

There is no real drink called this, but this is Deb and Pat's designated drink of choice for solstice, especially if it's a chilly night and you are around the fire.

There's nothing like a pot of coffee brewed on an open flame, and then into the steaming cup an addition of cream (the fat free is almost as good as the real), and a shot of almond liqueur. One is almost enough while sitting around the fire with the smoke and friends.

For kids or for those wishing to avoid the alcohol, if you use one of those yummy creamers with almond flavor it works just as well. After all, witches get high just from the gathering at solstice.

About Madeline Island
and Summer Solstice

Madeline Island is the largest of the Apostle Islands, located north of the Wisconsin Peninsula, although it is not included within the Apostle Islands National Lakeshore. It is the only island in the Apostle Island chain open to commercial development.

An Anishinaabe legend says that Great Spirit Gitche Manitou told the people to travel west to the place where the "food grows upon the water," which led them to the wild rice that grew in the marshes in nearby Chequamegon Bay.

The town of La Pointe is located on the southwestern tip of the island, with Grant's Point being the southeastern most point. Aside from its proximity to the federally managed National Lakeshore, Madeline Island also contains the Wisconsin Department of Natural Resources' Big Bay State Park, a 2,350-acre (9.5 square km) park on the south-central shore of the island. It is sometimes called Eagles' Nest for the bald eagles that make their nests in the tall pine trees on the cliffs. It encloses a large lagoon and a unique bog/dune ecosystem.

There is another, smaller park on the island called Big Bay Town Park that is closer to town, offers camping, and is free to the public. It has access to the longest beach on the island, and adjoins the state park.

The island itself is fourteen miles (21 km) long and three miles (5 km) wide. It is the only developed island of all the Apostle Islands, although there are lighthouses on many of the islands and small, preserved fishing communities on a few. The 2000 U.S. Census reported the permanent population of the island as two hundred forty-six, which does not include seasonal residents. The island is a popular vacation spot for people from all over the Midwest. The Golf Club sports a course designed by Robert Trent Jones that features double greens.

The island can be reached only by ferry during the summer months; in the winter, ice usually becomes too thick for ferry traffic. When ice conditions allow, the "ice road" officially opens to vehicle traffic from Bayfield across the frozen surface to Madeline Island. The ice road is traditionally marked by Christmas trees. If ice is too thin for automobile traffic but too thick for ferry traffic, access to the island is by airplane, snowmobile, and windsled only. The windsled often operates in early winter and spring. On the eastern end of the island is an enclave of the Bad River Indian Reservation of approximately 195 acres (0.79 km2).

The word solstice derives from Latin sol (sun) and sistere (to stand still).

The events in this story occur during and around the summer solstice. Worldwide, interpretation of the event has varied from culture to culture, but most recognize solstice as a sign of fertility – involving holidays, festivals, gatherings, rituals, or other celebrations around that time.

The summer solstice occurs exactly when the Earth's axial tilt is most inclined towards the sun at its maximum of 23° 26'. Except in the Polar Regions (where daylight is continuous for many months during the spring and summer), the day on which the summer solstice occurs is the day of the year with the longest period of daylight. So the seasonal significance of the summer solstice is in the reversal of the gradual shortening of nights and lengthening of days. The summer solstice occurs in June in the Northern Hemisphere and in December in the Southern Hemisphere.

It has recently become a popular belief in the United States that the meteorological season of summer begins with the astronomical phenomenon of the summer solstice. Other regions reckon the start of summer to the beginning of the month of the solstice, or even the month preceding it.

About the Council
of Thirteen Grandmothers

THE GRANDMOTHERS' MISSION STATEMENT

WE, THE INTERNATIONAL COUNCIL OF THIRTEEN INDIGENOUS
GRANDMOTHERS, represent a global alliance of prayer, education
and healing for our Mother Earth, all Her inhabitants, all the children,
and for the next seven generations to come.
We are deeply concerned with the unprecedented destruction
of our Mother Earth and the destruction of indigenous ways of life.
We believe the teachings of our ancestors will light our way through
an uncertain future.
We look to further our vision through the realization of projects
that protect our diverse cultures, lands, medicines, language
and ceremonial ways of prayer and through projects that educate
and nurture our children.

Website for Council of Thirteen Grandmothers:
www.grandmotherscouncil.com

To learn more or to visit Madeline Island:
www.madelineisland.com

DEAR FRIENDS

OF THE BEST FRIEND SERIES,

We are proud to announce that the series is now on e-books, but in order to get the word out, we need your help. Please e-mail to as many of your friends and relatives that all three books are now available for e-readers. Help us spread the news, so we can continue to write these charming little mysteries. Let us know on Facebook at *Best Friends Mysteries* that you have done so, and we'll thank you and send you a gift.

Some of you have asked whether we do writing seminars. Yes! We do writing retreats and book signings. For testimonials and more information, including fees, contact us at bestfriendsmysteries@gmail.com.

If you have a book club that is reading one of our series, invite us. If we can, we will come when you discuss it. It's great fun and a way to make your turn as book club hostess one your friends will always remember.

Thanks for your help.

Deb and Pat

CPSIA information can be obtained at www.ICGtesting.com
Printed in the USA
LVOW090553250412

279063LV00002B/2/P